ROUGHED UP

UP TO TROUBLE
BOOK 3

HANK EDWARDS

MITTEN GINGER MEDIA

CONTENTS

SUMMARY

A well-earned island vacation.
A missing boyfriend.
An out of jurisdiction agent racing against time.

Mark Beecher and FBI Special Agent Aaron Pearce are relaxing on the island of Barbados, filling their days with sun, surf, and each other. At a restaurant off the usual tourist route, Mark sees a woman he believes may be in danger and wants to try and help, however, Pearce reminds him they are not citizens and have no legal power on the island.

But Mark can't forget the woman, even after they return to the restaurant but are unable to find her again. Following an argument with Pearce about his inability to let it go, Mark slips away to investigate on his own. He locates the woman, but she is in trouble, and when Mark tries to intervene, he's taken captive as well. Mark is drugged and hidden away to await a sex slavery ring auction.

When Pearce is unable to locate Mark, he makes a report to the Barbados Royal Police Force. The detective he speaks with asks a lot of questions that make Pearce realize he's most likely the prime suspect in Mark's disappearance. With no official legal power on the island, Pearce begins his own investigation, determined to find and rescue Mark before the man he loves is taken off the island and lost forever.

Roughed Up ©2016 Hank Edwards
Cover design by Ron Perry Graphic Design
Book design and production by Hank Edwards
Editing by Sandra Rychel

First Publication, 2014

Big thanks to Ethan Day, who long ago suggested the seed of this story. What a difference a few years make, eh, my friend?

Huge, huge thanks to Sandra Rychel. Thank you for helping me keep Pearce as edgy and angry as we love him to be.

CHAPTER 1

The sand felt good beneath Mark's head. The cool, fine grains provided a stark contrast to the scratch of Pearce's stubble against Mark's lips as they kissed. Waves rolled up on the beach several yards away, and somewhere even farther off—back at the hotel bar, most likely—a woman's loud, drunken laugh floated on the breeze. An hour ago they had watched the sunset from a small table in the hotel bar while eating shrimp and downing drink specials. Finally Pearce had suggested a moonlit walk on the beach, and Mark had happily agreed.

"You taste like mango," Pearce said between kisses.

"Those margaritas you kept pushing on me," Mark replied.

"I seem to remember you placing those orders," Pearce murmured, then pushed his tongue into Mark's mouth in a slow, sensual kiss. He pressed a palm against Mark's erection, still trapped within his board shorts, and they moaned together.

Pearce ducked his head to put his lips right next to Mark's ear and whispered, "Want you." He followed that up by corkscrewing his tongue into the sensitive canal.

"Me too," Mark said around a gasp. "God, I love when you do that."

Pearce slipped his hand up the leg of Mark's shorts to grope his balls and his throbbing cock.

Mark pulled away and smiled in nervous surprise at Pearce before turning to look up and down the beach. Barbados had laws against homosexual behavior, a fact that would have made Mark steer clear of a trip here. But it had also been the most affordable tropical island trip he had been able to find, and they had really, really needed to get away. He focused on Pearce and said in a low voice, "You want to do it here? On the beach?"

Pearce checked out the beach as well, then grinned like a mischievous frat boy when he met Mark's gaze again. "There's no one around. Besides, we're on an island vacation; it's a rule that we have to have sex on the beach at some point."

"Oh, is that a rule?" Mark chuckled. "I guess I missed hearing that when we checked in."

"I definitely heard it." Pearce kissed him. "I think the woman said it's required two times at least." Another kiss. "In different positions."

Mark felt a little light-headed, mostly from the mango margaritas he'd drunk at the hotel bar, but also from the persuasion of Pearce's kisses. Goddamn, but Pearce could kiss. He found a shred of resistance left and pulled back to say, "You know Barbados has strict laws against homosexual acts."

"Yeah?" Pearce grumbled. "So did my prom date's brother, but he blew me behind the school."

Mark shook his head. "What does that have to do with anything we're discussing?"

"God, you're so wet," Pearce whispered, smearing the precum around the head of Mark's cock with his index finger, his lips just brushing Mark's. "Let's flip-flop right here. You fuck me, and then

I'll fuck you." Another kiss, stronger, hungrier. "I want your cock in my ass. I want to feel your cum drip down my thigh while we walk back to the room."

Mark's cock jumped in Pearce's fist at the image he planted in his head.

"You're killing me," he said.

"Come on. It's our first vacation together."

Mark smiled up at him. "You mean your trip to Detroit at the beginning of the year wasn't a vacation?"

Pearce pulled his hand from Mark's shorts, grabbed him by the shoulder, and rolled them both over so Mark lay on top.

"No," Pearce said and held Mark's head between his hands, eyes shifting as he studied Mark's face. "I think it was fate."

Fuck. Pearce really knew how to get to him. When the man said romantic things like that, Mark melted. And Pearce knew it, the bastard.

"You are such a liar," Mark said and kissed him hard.

"Not at all," Pearce managed before their tongues tangled together.

Pearce lifted his hips and reached down to slide off his shorts. He hadn't worn underwear since they'd arrived—neither of them had—and the hot, solid length of his cock pressed against Mark's hip. Mark reached down to take hold of it, squeezed it, and then lifted his hips to allow Pearce to remove his shorts as well.

The ocean breeze on his bare ass excited Mark, but he was still nervous and broke their kiss to rise up and peer each way along the beach. No one in sight. Did people in Barbados just sit in bars and drink at night? No one walked the beach?

"And you claimed you'd never had sex in public before." Pearce stroked Mark's cock. "You're hard as rock."

"You're a bad influence."

Pearce grinned up at him before unbuttoning Mark's camp shirt. "Bet you say that to all the FBI agents you fuck."

Mark shrugged out of his shirt, then lowered his head to take Pearce's dick between his lips. The familiar taste—a mix of sweat, soap, and that special spice that was uniquely Aaron Pearce—surged along his tongue. Mark paused, his mouth filled with Pearce's cock and the ocean breeze trailing over his bare skin. The waves continued their sonorous rolls, and the quiet strains of a reggae band floated from somewhere down the beach.

"Get your cock up here," Pearce demanded, his voice husky with lust.

In a moment Mark had shifted position, and they lay face to crotch, sucking each other. Mark worked a hand between Pearce's legs and circled the soft, wrinkled skin of Pearce's hole with his index finger. Pearce moaned encouragement, lifted his leg to let him farther in, and Mark paused to suck his finger, then pushed in to the first knuckle.

"Oh, fuck yeah," Pearce said. He stroked Mark's prick. "Get your finger in me."

Mark sucked Pearce's cock and finger fucked him, adding a second finger now and then to stretch him open.

Pearce groaned and sighed, then said in deep voice, "Fuck me."

Needing no further invitation, Mark pushed Pearce onto his back and positioned himself between the man's legs.

"Lube's in the pocket of my shorts," Pearce said.

Mark narrowed his eyes. "Did you plan this?"

"Abso-fuckin'-lutely. Now slick up that dick and put it in me."

They both laughed as Mark patted Pearce's discarded shorts, found the small tube of slick, and popped open the cap.

"For God's sake, don't get any sand in it," Pearce said.

Mark pouted at him. "Oh, poor, sensitive FBI agent. Would sand in your ass make you cry?"

Pearce glared at him, the tan of his face washed out by the moonlight. "You're asking for it, Beecher."

"Damn right I am. Hold still."

Mark got into position, touched the gleaming tip of his cock to Pearce's hole, and pushed. They were beyond condoms now, both committed to their relationship, and the hot clutch of Pearce's body around Mark's bare skin made him moan.

"Aaron," Mark whispered, using Pearce's first name as he moved deeper into him. "Dear God, I love you." He leaned down for a kiss.

"I love you too. Now fuck me."

Mark braced himself with hands planted in the sand at either side of Pearce and pumped his hips. The excitement of fucking outside had him hypersensitive to everything around him, including the feeling of being bare inside Pearce. His orgasm curled in the familiar spot deep inside him, his balls tightening and his hips driving as if of their own accord. As he thrust into Pearce, Mark studied his lover in the white moonlight, let his gaze move over his handsome, stubbled face, down to the broad chest covered with dark hair. He rose up and took hold of Pearce's ankles, adjusting his position to pump faster.

"Fuck yeah," Pearce said. "Yeah, that's it."

A moment later, he felt the flash fire of orgasm, and he grunted quietly with each pulse as he came inside Pearce's ass. Sweat ran down his face, though the night breeze was cool, and he kissed Pearce softly on the lips as he eased out of him.

"Mango margaritas," Pearce said and reached to pull Mark back for another kiss. "I'll have to remember that."

Mark laughed, then gasped when Pearce flipped him onto his back and knelt between his legs. Pearce's hard cock stuck straight out to point at Mark as if he'd been selected. And in a way he had been.

"My turn," Pearce whispered in Mark's ear. "Ready?"

In response, Mark lifted his legs and grabbed the backs of his knees. Pearce groaned, looked both ways along the beach once more to be sure they were alone, and then lubed up his cock and slid it home.

Mark stared up at the stars as Pearce entered him. They were blurry—he'd left his glasses back in the room—but he really wanted to remember this moment. He focused on his other senses instead: the sound and smell of the ocean and the soft, fine sand against his back as Pearce pushed into him. Mark thought he would never tire of the burn as his muscles stretched to accommodate Pearce's girth —and the hot, slick-tacky mix of lube and sweat that worked in tandem to give Pearce the ease and friction needed to fuck him good and deep.

Shifting his gaze to Pearce's face, Mark found him staring and smiled. "God, that's amazing."

"Like it?"

"Yeah." Mark drew in a breath as Pearce's stroke shifted and the broad head of his cock skimmed his prostate. "Oh, like that."

"I feel it." Pearce nodded. "Damn, I'm close."

"Do it," Mark whispered. "Fill me up."

Pearce tightened his grip on Mark's ankles, and he tipped his head back, eyes squeezed tight as he moved even faster, pounding his cock into Mark. It skimmed across his prostate several times in a row, and Mark reached down to stroke his cock, hard once again.

"Coming." Pearce grunted as he slowed his strokes to a final, deep thrust. The orgasm pulsed through Pearce's entire body, and as he shifted in the moonlight, Mark could see the scar on his right shoulder, where he'd been stabbed back in Detroit.

"Stay inside me," Mark said. "I love having you inside me." He moved his hand fast, faster still, and soon he shivered on the cool sand as he came across his belly.

"So hot," Pearce whispered as he slipped out of him. He trailed his fingers through the puddles of cum and then lifted them to his lips to suck them clean. "Salty."

Mark smiled up at him. "Shall we clean off in the ocean?"

Pearce pretended to be shocked. "What would the fish think?"

They laughed together, and Pearce helped Mark to his feet. They raced to the water, Pearce's long legs taking him in the lead. The water was cool, and Mark let out a gasp when it touched his ankles, but then he saw the white flash of Pearce's bare ass in the moonlight ahead of him, and he dived in.

For several minutes they splashed each other, came together to kiss and grope, and then broke apart for more splashing. Finally Mark pushed away and swam back to shore, where he trudged up to the pile of their clothes, Pearce right behind him.

As they dressed, they touched and stroked each other, pausing for one more kiss beneath the moon and stars before linking hands and turning toward the hotel. Sand was stuck to his legs and feet, and Mark knew he would be hungover in the morning, but he felt mellow and calm after fucking and swimming, and he stole glances at Pearce as they walked.

"Want to go into town tomorrow?" Mark asked.

"If we can end the day out here on the beach again, absolutely," Pearce replied.

A group of people staggered down the steps from the hotel bar and onto the sand a few yards ahead of them, and Mark pulled his fingers free of Pearce's grip. The group shouted greetings, which they returned, and then Mark preceded Pearce up the steps toward the pool area and the beach entrance of their hotel.

CHAPTER 2

The wind was up, making it more difficult than Pearce had expected to control the rental motor scooter. He watched Mark, riding on his own scooter ahead of him, swerve from one side of the road to the other, the wind buffeting him and making Pearce's pulse jump. He wanted to shout for Mark to slow down, ease up on the damn throttle, but he knew the words would just get lost in the wind. To his left, the Caribbean Sea thrashed against the shore, dousing them with foam and sprays of salt water. Hard to believe they had had sex on the beach last night without freezing their asses off.

His cock pulsed at the memory of being on the beach with Mark, inside Mark, and he had to shake his head. Had he really been that much more relaxed last night? Or maybe he'd just been much less sober than he was currently.

As if drawn by Pearce's thoughts, Mark looked back over his shoulder and flashed a sexy smile. Pearce checked to make sure they were unobserved before he reached down to lift a leg of his shorts and show Mark he wasn't wearing underwear. Mark let out a shocked laugh, and even from his distance, Pearce could tell

Mark was blushing. Not bad if Pearce could still make his lover blush.

Lover. There was a foreign word if ever Pearce heard one. How had he managed to snag a lover? Better yet, how had Mark managed to snag *him*? Pearce had always considered himself something of a misanthrope, a loner who shunned the personal connections and trappings of relationships. And yet here he was, playing tag on a motor scooter around the island of Barbados with his live-in lover.

What in the fucking hell was wrong with this picture?

Pearce had to smirk to himself and admit, absolutely nothing.

They puttered past the Garrison Savannah horse-racing track and continued riding along the road, the beach of Carlisle Bay between them and the sea, until they reached the city limits of Bridgetown. Suddenly they were in traffic, heavier than Pearce was comfortable for them to be surrounded by, and he pressed the button for his horn to get Mark's attention, cursing at the high-pitched beep that drew the attention of everyone around him and made them smirk. Just another couple of tourists. When Mark looked back at him, Pearce gestured for him to pull over and was relieved when Mark actually took the suggestion.

Pearce followed as Mark rolled the scooter around a corner onto a side street, where they both eased to a stop at the curb.

"Wasn't that awesome?" Mark's smile was bright and his hair tousled. "Feeling the spray from the ocean and the wind?" His cheeks and nose were pink with sunburn, and Pearce wanted to haul him off behind a building and fuck him hard and deep.

"You're quite the daredevil on that scooter," Pearce said, trying not to sound like he was throwing ice water on Mark's fun, which was precisely what he felt like he needed to do.

Mark smiled down at the scooter between his legs with something close to puppy love. "It's hard not to be. These little scooters are so nimble and fun. I'd love to have one back home in DC."

Pearce shook his head, unable to stop himself from saying, "In all that heavy traffic? You'd be run off the road in a week."

With a shrug Mark turned away, but not before Pearce saw a slight flinch flash across his face. He mentally cursed himself. Why couldn't he just let Mark have some fun? Here he was in Barbados, his left arm only a week out of a cast, relaxed and happy after an intense showdown back in DC, and Pearce had to grind it down.

"But you know," Pearce offered, trying to make amends, "I'm sure you'd fix an orange flag or something to the back to announce yourself in traffic."

Mark turned to grin at him, but it didn't have the same wattage as his earlier smile, and Pearce felt a cold trickle of guilt seep into his chest as Mark said, "Yeah. Something to make me stand out." Mark stood up, his feet at either side of the scooter, and inspected their surroundings. "I don't see many tourist-type places in this area." He turned back to Pearce and waggled his eyebrows. "I kind of like it. Do you want to head down this road a bit?"

Pearce shrugged and nodded. "Yeah. For a little while. But I'm going to be hungry soon. It's almost beer o'clock."

Mark let out a sigh, and the smile that followed appeared a little less strained, so Pearce chalked one up for himself before pressing the scooter's starter button. He followed Mark along the road, the sea falling farther behind them. A quiet sense of unease threaded into his gut, but he wanted Mark to enjoy the outing—one of two they could afford—so Pearce stayed mum and kept an eye out for trouble. His attention sharpened to the point that every car behind or rolling toward them became a possible threat.

The flash of a turn signal ahead snapped Pearce's focus back to Mark, and he rounded the corner after him, then honked the horn again, motioning for Mark to pull over.

"Where you headed?" Pearce asked after they had shut down the engines.

Mark shrugged. "I don't know. Just kind of touring the city, seeing what's here."

"Oh, okay." Pearce tried to appear laid-back, though his FBI instincts grumbled unhappily inside him. He'd heard horror stories about tourists taking one wrong turn and ending up mugged or murdered. The neighborhoods could change quickly on a condensed island.

Mark stared at him a moment, and Pearce could almost hear the gears and pulleys in Mark's brain grinding as he tried to find a way to tell him to relax without starting an argument.

"You okay back there?" Mark asked.

Pearce nodded. "Yeah, why?"

"Just wanted to be sure. You seem a little…" Mark narrowed his eyes, as if assessing him. "Jumpy, I guess. Would you rather we head back to the hotel and eat lunch there?"

Pearce had to bite back the resounding *yes* that practically crawled up the back of his throat. Instead he simply shook his head and tried like hell to appear relaxed and innocent. He was supposed to be the daredevil of this relationship and Mark the down-to-earth anchor. "No, not at all. I just wanted to see if you had a destination in mind."

"Not really," Mark said. "Thought we'd sightsee. That's all. The streets off the beaten path, you know? Away from the bus tours and tourist traps."

"Okay, sure." Pearce couldn't help adding, "I just don't want to get too far off that beaten path."

A wry smile sapped some of the light from Mark's gaze. "You the same guy who convinced me to fuck on the beach last night?"

Pearce knew Mark had a point, and he hesitated, considering his actions and how to respond. What was different from last night? About five or six strong drinks, that was what. He turned back and said, "Well, that was drunk Pearce. Right now I'm just slightly hungover Pearce, who understands he's in a foreign country."

Mark nodded. "I see." He started his scooter once again and then said over the noise of the tiny engine, "Just relax, Agent Pearce. You're on vacation."

Mark puttered away before Pearce could reply, and he cursed himself again before starting his scooter and following.

The houses along the side of the road thinned out, replaced by small businesses and warehouses. Pearce noticed the two of them received some long, hard stares as they motored by, and his paranoia amped up even more. Mark continued to roll along the street, blond hair blowing back from his forehead, bright-colored button-down shirt flapping around his toned torso. Pearce followed, trying to keep his gaze fixed on Mark's back and not jumping around between potential threats.

Not much farther along the road, Mark flicked on a turn signal and motored into a parking lot layered with bright white gravel stones. Several cars were parked in a row, and Mark and Pearce pulled their scooters up alongside one of the vehicles and shut off the engines.

Mark smiled at him and nodded at the building before them. "What do you think?"

It was a long, narrow building made of cinder block and painted white to match the gravel. A sign on the well-tended lawn out front proclaimed it as THE FLYING FISH EATERY. Pearce looked over his shoulder at a small bar that stood directly across the shared parking lot. Called THE BRIDGETOWN BAR, its wood siding was faded and worn by the elements, down to a dirty shade of white, much dingier than the restaurant's cinder block paint job or even the gravel stones they had parked on. A young Bajan man sat on the porch watching them, a toothpick jutting out from the corner of his mouth, his feet resting on the railing.

Pearce turned back to the Flying Fish Eatery again and shrugged. "Looks authentic."

Mark sighed. "That's it?" He waved a hand at the restaurant. "Come on. With a name like that? Flying fish! We're in Barbados. We have to try flying fish."

Pearce cocked his head. "Do they fly onto the plate?"

"No, they don't fly onto the plate. But they have small wings and can fly short distances out of the water. It's a local delicacy here in Barbados." Mark raised his eyebrows. "You up for it?"

Pearce nodded, but his attention strayed back to the man on the porch of the bar. "Yeah, sure, sounds good."

Mark followed Pearce's gaze toward the bar and said, "Come on, let's go inside. Don't make me remind you yet again that we're on vacation." Mark got off the scooter and headed for the restaurant, saying over his shoulder, "Move your ass, Agent Pearce."

Pearce turned away from the stare-down with the man on the porch, sighed, and grumbled, "Hardheaded chef." But he got off the scooter and followed Mark up the cement path to the door. "I'll go inside, but if there's a seagull sitting in there, or some other animal, I'm out. Got it?"

Mark laughed. "Got it."

Pearce wasn't going to regret giving in to Mark on this, because his stomach had been rumbling since they'd reached the city limits. He was hungry, but he wasn't yet sold on flying fish. He considered himself open to most any type of food, but there were just some things that shouldn't be cooked and served as a meal.

At the door to the restaurant, Pearce turned to look across the parking lot at the man on the porch. Something about him—was it is his posture? his expression?—sent a ping like sonar through Pearce's agent instincts. There was a threatening air about the man, and Pearce wondered if their scooters would still be there when they came out. The man stared back at Pearce a moment before shifting his gaze away.

The aroma of spices, fried food, and yeast made Pearce's mouth water as he trailed Mark through the door, and he put all considerations of the man at the bar out of his mind as he thought that maybe this place wouldn't be so bad after all.

CHAPTER 3

Mark stopped just inside the door of the Flying Fish Eatery and took a deep breath, inhaling the heady smell of food being cooked. He detected onion, citrus, and what he thought might be a touch of curry—an interesting mix of spices. Half the tables were occupied, and when a broad-hipped waitress pushed out of the kitchen door, she flashed a bright smile and called, "Have a seat at any open table, young sirs. I'll be with you in a breeze."

Mark waved in response and led the way to a table near the opposite end of the restaurant. After sitting down, he assessed Pearce's demeanor and could tell he was strung tight with tension. He tried to push calming thoughts toward Pearce as he watched him examine every other couple in the place. Even though Mark felt relaxed and was excited to try some local food, he did notice that both of them had automatically put their backs to the wall to be able to see the room. They had been through enough together—in Detroit and again in Washington, DC—to know the basics of staying safe. He smiled at Pearce and tried to think of some way to make this up to him back at the room, but it was tough to find a position or act they hadn't done already.

The waitress approached, her smile friendly and her expression open. As she told them about the specials, her slight English accent made everything sound even better, and Mark was glad when Pearce joked with her about the temperature of the beer, making sure they served it cold here in Barbados. After some discussion about menu items, they both decided to try the flying fish, battered, then flash fried and served with a side of *cou-cou*, which the waitress explained as a cornmeal and okra mix.

"Thank you," Mark said, leaning back in his chair after the waitress had walked off.

"For what?" Pearce asked.

"Coming in here with me, trying the flying fish. I appreciate it."

"Well, I can't have you wasting away while we're on vacation," Pearce said. "How would that look to all our friends back home?"

"Do we have friends back home?" Mark had meant it as a joke but knew the minute the last word left his lips that it might not be well received. And from the expression on Pearce's face, his instinct proved correct.

"What's that mean?" Pearce asked as a muscle in his jaw ticked.

"It doesn't mean anything. It was just a joke. That's all."

"Look, I know we don't go out a lot." Pearce's tone grew defensive. "We don't socialize with many people. But I figured you knew what you were getting into when you agreed to move to DC with me."

A tiny cold spot formed in the center of Mark's chest, like a very small, angry fist made of ice, and he tried to see a way to backpedal. Things had been going so well, and here he had to go and make a stupid comment and fuck up the afternoon. Were relationships always this difficult?

"It was just a flippant comment, okay? Please don't read anything into it. I was just making a joke." Mark leaned in closer over the table and lowered his voice. "I love you. I don't want anything to change between us. I love us the way we are, here in Barbados or back home in DC."

Pearce sat back as the waitress approached with a water pitcher and topped off their glasses. She chatted with them a little, asking where they were from, how long they planned to stay in Barbados, and all the while Mark wished she would just leave them alone so he could finish putting things right with Pearce.

When the waitress finally turned to attend to another table, Mark caught Pearce's eye and asked, "Are we okay now?"

He got a quick nod in response, but Mark wasn't reassured by the way Pearce shifted his gaze away. Before he could say another word, the waitress came back with their plates of food. She stood by the table, hands clasped before her, waiting for them to take their first bites. Mark gathered a bite of fish and cou-cou onto his fork, slipped it in his mouth, and let it rest on his tongue. The fish was firm with a light flavor, and the combination of the spices—including a touch of heat from a cayenne pepper, if his taste buds weren't lying—and the cou-cou coated with a tangy red sauce made him sigh.

"It's good?" the waitress asked.

Mark smiled up at her and nodded. "It's very good."

She looked at Pearce. "You like it too?"

Mark watched as Pearce took his first bite and thoughtfully chewed. Pearce liked medium-heat Thai food, so Mark thought he would appreciate the flavor, and he was relieved when Pearce sat back and grinned.

"I like it," Pearce assured her.

She beamed. "Best flying fish and cou-cou on the island. You can bet the house on that."

She laughed as she walked away, and they both resumed eating. After a few more bites of food, Mark asked, "We're okay?"

Pearce hesitated, then gave him a nod. "I'm okay if you are."

"Of course I'm okay," Mark said. "I'm eating good food on a tropical island with my handsome man. How much better can it get?"

"Yeah, good point." Pearce went back to his meal, but not before Mark saw him smirk.

After they had cleaned their plates and paid the bill, Mark followed Pearce out the door, his lips tingling from the spicy finish of the cou-cou sauce. The gravel crunched beneath their flip-flops as they crossed to their scooters, and off in the distance Mark could hear seagulls crying.

"The porch guard has a following," Pearce said in a low voice.

"What?" Mark looked up at the bar that squatted on the other side of the parking lot, and slowed his walk as his gaze locked with that of a young Caucasian girl. She had long blonde hair that lay straight and limp down past her shoulders. Dark circles hung beneath her eyes, and she shifted her gaze between Mark and the man who sat in the chair on the porch. Two other girls stood on the other side of the porch, leaning on the railing and staring off across the street. The blonde girl stared at Mark, and he could see her chewing one corner of her lower lip.

"Hey," Pearce said.

"What?" Mark blinked at him. "Sorry. Did you say something?"

Pearce checked out the girl a moment before turning his attention back to Mark. "What's got you distracted?"

"Nothing." Mark looked at the girl again, noticing that the man sitting behind her had now fixed him with a cold stare. Mark shivered when he met the man's gaze, and quickly turned away. There was something about that girl, something about her face and expression that triggered a sense of déjà vu.

Then it came back to him. Summer Barrington, a girl who had been a senior in his high school when he had been a sophomore. She had gone on a senior trip to a Caribbean island at the end of the school year with a group of friends and never came home. That had been back in 2000, five years before the Natalee Holloway case called attention to the dangers of American girls traveling alone. Mark could recall the posters in the school hallways those last two weeks of classes, all with Summer's smiling senior photo and the promises, the hopes, that she would be found.

But she never had been found, had she? He didn't think so. Over the summer, he had read a few newspaper articles about the case, but he didn't think Summer or her body had ever been recovered. He remembered thinking back then how horrible it would be for a parent to live with never knowing what happened to their child.

Mark studied the girl. She was thin—very thin—and as Mark watched, she raked her nails back and forth along her left arm, under the long sleeve of a lightweight pullover.

"That girl," Mark said and turned to Pearce. "The blonde on the porch."

Pearce checked out the girl in a quick glance. "Yeah? You think she's a prostitute?"

"No. Well, not sure. Probably. It's just that she reminds me of a girl back home. Someone from my high school."

"You're talking about the one that looks like an addict?"

"Yeah. She's been staring over here since we came out."

"Maybe we're the only white guys she's seen in a while," Pearce suggested.

"Could be." Mark glanced at the girl again and was startled when the man sitting behind her abruptly stood up and glared at him. Mark turned away, his heart racing as he sat on his scooter.

"So what's the story with this girl back home?" Pearce asked. "The one she reminds you about."

"She went on a senior trip to one of the islands here in the Caribbean and didn't come home." Mark nodded as Pearce's face tightened. "This was in 2000, before Natalee Holloway."

"Parents never found out what happened?"

Mark shook his head. "Not that I heard about. She was two years ahead of me in school."

Pearce dropped his gaze and then lifted his head with a surprised expression. "Damn, you're that much younger than me?"

Mark grinned. "I'm just a young cub compared to you, old man."

Pearce flinched and mounted his scooter. "Ouch."

Mark started his scooter and risked a final glance back at the girl. He noted her blue eyes wide with fear, her fingers gripping the rail, and her lips moving as she mouthed something to him. Mark squinted as he tried to make out what she might be saying, but then the man behind her cuffed her hard on the back of the head and turned to stride toward the steps down to the cement path. The man's intention was clear: he was coming to have a talk with them —most likely more than that—and Mark turned away and twisted the throttle to pull quickly out of the lot.

CHAPTER 4

Pearce was more relaxed on the return trip and enjoyed the ride. He led the way this time, keeping his speed slow and steady as he followed the road that circled Barbados. The blue water stretched out from the white-sand beaches, where people lay on towels or stood talking and laughing, and the cloudless sky overhead rained sunshine over them. By the time they returned the scooters to the rental booth, Pearce noticed that Mark's edginess over the blonde girl seemed to have faded. As they walked toward the hotel entrance—and especially in the elevator on the way up to their floor—they joked about flying fish and the motor scooters, touching like giddy college freshmen on a first date, and Pearce felt himself thoroughly relaxed once again.

Mark's comment about their lack of friends back home still buzzed inside his head, bothersome like a mosquito in the room when he might be trying to sleep, but he was determined to let it go. Mark hadn't meant anything by it—at least he didn't *think* Mark had meant anything by it—but it was something to consider. Pearce didn't have many friends outside the FBI. He had always preferred the anonymity of the bar scene and one-night stands, avoiding the messy entanglements of friendships or relationships. And now here he was, all tangled up in a relationship, and he had no idea what he was doing and no friends to talk with about the ins and outs of the emotional tango of romance.

But he knew what he wanted to do right now—with Mark—and it was what he did best. Some might say he put the physical aspects of his associations above any emotional ties, but he had been working on opening up more to Mark. It was difficult at times—okay, most times—but the deeper connection they'd forged since Mark had moved in with him made the sex even better. Pearce knew where Mark liked to be touched, knew what would get him hot and what would push him right over the edge. And the same held true for Mark about him.

Mark was very much Pearce's type, and Pearce loved having free rein to touch, kiss, and suck whatever area of Mark's body he wanted. With this in mind, once Pearce closed the door to their room, he pulled Mark against him for a hot, deep kiss. Mark's hard-on pressed against his thigh, making Pearce's erection jump in anticipation. They broke apart long enough to strip off their shirts before resuming the kiss. Pearce slid his tongue into Mark's mouth, rolled it around Mark's tongue, and skimmed it along the edge of his teeth. He ran his hands up and down Mark's back, then brought them around front to slide his fingers through the hair on Mark's chest until he came to his nipples. Pearce pinched the hard points and rolled them between his thumbs and forefingers.

"Oh my God, you make me so fucking hot," Mark said with a moan.

"Yeah, and I'm standing here all calm and shit," Pearce said, and Mark smacked his upper arm. "Hey! What was that for?"

"You are a complete smart-ass."

"What's that? You want to eat my ass?" Pearce sighed and took a step back to push his shorts down. His cock bobbed before him, the head slick with precum, and he stroked it a couple of times before turning his back to Mark and bending forward with his hands on his knees. "Go at it, Scooter Boy."

He felt Mark squeeze the hairy swells of his ass cheeks. A finger trailed slowly down the crack of his ass and circled the furrows of his anus. Pearce pushed back against Mark's finger, groaning when it slipped just inside the threshold of his hole.

"You like that, huh?" Mark's voice was low and tinged with lust.

"Yeah, I do."

"Want more?"

"I want your tongue up there first," Pearce said. "Stop teasing me, and eat my hole."

Mark knelt behind him, his cock standing straight out from the trimmed patch of blond pubic hair to poke between Pearce's legs. He gripped Pearce's ass cheeks and spread them wide, kneading the muscles hard. At the flicker of touch from Mark's tongue, Pearce closed his eyes and sighed.

With a slow, steady pace, Mark ran the tip of his tongue around the creases of Pearce's anus, dipping it into the center when he reached the top. He pushed in deeper each time until, finally, he had his mouth pressed tight against Pearce, his tongue spiking into the damp center of him.

Pearce couldn't help talking. "Oh fuck, that's it. Get your tongue in me."

Mark licked and sucked and licked some more, leaving Pearce's hole wet and eager for something bigger.

"That is so fucking hot," Mark said after sitting back and circling his finger around the slick ridges of muscle.

"Fuck me," Pearce practically pleaded. "I want your cock inside me."

"In good time," Mark teased. He stood up and pushed Pearce toward the bed. "On your back, Agent."

Pearce felt a quiver of excitement in his belly as he stretched out across the bed. As much as he liked to be in control of situations, he did enjoy it when Mark told him what to do. He stroked himself, but Mark slapped his hand away, then climbed onto the bed, turned his back to Pearce, and straddled his face. Pearce found himself staring up at Mark's balls and ass and pulled him down. He spread Mark's ass cheeks and feasted on the pink pucker of his hole, tasting his sweat and smelling his musky, male scent. Mark lifted Pearce's legs and lowered his head to continue rimming him, Pearce groaning his encouragement.

Mark slid one finger into the depths of Pearce's ass, his spit easing the burn of entry. Fucking Pearce slowly with one finger, Mark then added a second, pushing a moan up from Pearce's gut as he moved his fingers faster. Pearce pulled his mouth off Mark's ass, slid a finger into him, then heard the groan he expected.

They finger fucked each other for a while, speeding up, then slowing down, using one finger, then two, sometimes three, and then back to one. There were no appointments or work schedules to get in their way, no time limit to their exploration of each other's bodies, just the impatient throb of their cocks as precum dribbled down the shafts. Pearce had been with Mark longer than anyone else he had ever dated; he knew every inch of Mark—every birthmark and scar, every dimple and curve. And even with the terrain of Mark's body mapped out in his mind, Pearce still wanted to revel in it, soak it up. He liked the sweat-damp touch of Mark's hands, the long reach of his fingers, the expressive sighs and moans he earned with his actions.

Mark shifted position and took Pearce in his mouth as he continued to finger fuck him. Pearce let out a grunt in surprise. He was close—so close—but he didn't want to come just yet. He wanted, *needed*, more. More time to explore his lover, please his lover, and most of all, more of Mark. Only now he wanted to feel Mark buried inside him.

Mark lifted his head, stroking Pearce's length as he moved to be able to smirk at him. "Think you're ready for me now, Agent Pearce?"

Pearce faked a yawn and let his gaze drift away from Mark. "Nah. I'm kind of tired now. You took too long."

"That's it," Mark said through a laugh and quickly got to his knees on the mattress.

"Oh, now you want to fuck me?" Pearce gave a heavy sigh, as though the thought of it exhausted him. "I guess I can get into it."

"You'll get into it, all right," Mark assured him as he moved into place between Pearce's legs. He picked up the lube he must have grabbed from the nightstand when Pearce got on the bed, and slicked himself up. Pearce felt the hot touch of Mark's cock against his hole, followed by the steady push of his entry, and he tilted his head back to groan. In one slow, steady push, Mark slid into him. The familiar feeling of fullness made Pearce gasp, and he reached out to pull Mark down for a kiss.

"I love you," Pearce said.

"I love you too," Mark replied. Then he pulled back his hips and started to fuck him.

Mark held Pearce's ankles tight as he moved his hips fast, then faster still. Just as Pearce felt his orgasm drawing close, however, Mark stopped and pulled out. Before Pearce could ask what he was doing, Mark lifted Pearce's legs high, raising his hips and lower back off the mattress. Mark stood on the bed to tip Pearce's legs over his head, and then he pushed his cock down and slid into him once again.

"Oh, fuck yeah," Pearce managed as Mark bounced on the mattress and pounded down into him. "Pile drive that hole."

Sweat ran down Mark's face, and the scent of their sex filled the room. Pearce balanced himself on the mattress with his shoulders and outstretched arms as Mark fucked him hard and deep, his cock raking across Pearce's prostate with each stroke. In moments Pearce was gone, tumbling over into orgasm and reaching up to stroke himself to completion. His cum splattered his face, hot and thick, and he licked off what he could reach with his tongue, savoring the briny taste of himself.

"Coming," Mark gasped. "I'm coming." He bounced hard on the mattress a few more times, head back, eyes closed as he emptied himself inside Pearce's body.

Spent, they collapsed on the bed, and Pearce pulled Mark in close for a sticky, salty kiss.

Mark smiled and moved to lick some of the cum off his face. "I'm usually the one getting a Pearce facial."

Pearce grinned. "Thought I'd see how it felt."

"What did you think?"

"Better than I imagined. I think my skin looks a lot younger."

They laughed together, and Pearce held him closer still, enjoying the sweaty, sticky touch of his skin. More kisses, softer now, and then they drifted off to sleep.

CHAPTER 5

A thump followed by cursing woke Mark from a deep, contented sleep. He sat up in bed, eyes narrowed as he peered around the dimly lit room. Where was he? Who was with him?

Then he remembered. Barbados. He was with Pearce, well, Aaron. It was tough sometimes to think of him as just Aaron; Pearce seemed to sum the man up so perfectly. Either way, Pearce wasn't in bed with him. "Aaron?"

"Yeah, it's me," came the grumbled reply.

Mark squinted across the shadowed room. He could see Pearce's form hunched over near the door "What's going on?" Mark reached out to turn on the bedside lamp and then fumbled his glasses out of their case. When he looked back at Pearce, he could see the man was nude and crouched near the door, rubbing his shin.

Pearce blinked up at him in the lamplight with an annoyed expression. "I stepped on your goddamn flip-flop by the door and barked my shin on this chair."

A cool, cautious feeling of regret and guilt seeped into Mark's gut. Pearce had asked him more than once not to just leave his shoes lying in the middle of the floor. He screwed up his face into what he hoped came across as a sincere apology and said, "Sorry. I was just so turned on when we got home I stepped out of them."

"Yeah, I know. I just wish you'd be more careful. You do this same thing at home." Pearce rubbed his shin a little more before he picked up one of the offending flip-flops and inspected the bottom. "What's this all about?" He held it up so Mark could see the bottom where a tab meant to keep plastic bags closed secured the rubber button of the toe separator.

Mark shrugged. "I just bought those fucking flip-flops yesterday, and the button holding the strap in place pulled out of the sole. When we were at breakfast yesterday, I was talking to Salvador as he was unwrapping bagels, and I saw the tab and remembered seeing the way to fix it on the Internet."

Pearce shook his head as he straightened up. "You cooks band together to make the world a better place all the time?"

A quiet breath of relief slipped from Mark's lips. The storm of Pearce's temper had passed—again—and he was able to smile as he replied, "We're both actually chefs, you know, not cooks. I was a station chef back in Detroit, and Salvador's an omelet station chef."

"Chef, cook, tomato, tomahto," Pearce grumbled before tossing the flip-flop aside. "Try to keep your shoes out of the middle of the floor, okay? Please?"

Mark nodded before turning away to slide out of bed. "I will. Sorry." As he headed for the bathroom, Mark met up with Pearce and stopped to give him a soft kiss. "Thanks for a fun afternoon."

"You sure you had fun?"

Mark frowned at him. "What do you mean?"

"While we were sleeping, you seemed to be having some bad dreams. You shouted a couple of times, loud enough to wake me up."

"Oh?" Mark dropped his gaze to stare at the carpet, trying to remember. "I shouted?"

"Yeah," Pearce said. "Scared the crap out of me, honestly. Brought me right up out of a sound sleep."

A hazy memory of the dream rolled to the surface in Mark's mind. "Oh wow. I'm sorry. I kind of remember something, now that you mention it. That girl from the bar was in it. She was in trouble, and I tried to help her, but I kept losing sight of her in the bar."

Pearce looked at him in silence a long moment and then softly touched his cheek. "She really bothered you, didn't she?"

"Yeah, she did. I guess more than I realized." Mark turned his head to place a kiss in the warm, damp center of Pearce's palm. He walked around him and into the bathroom, leaving the door open as he peed. "Situations like that really bother me," he said over the sound of his stream. "I got the feeling there was something not right about it, you know? But what can we do? It makes me feel so fucking helpless."

He finished, washed up, and walked back into the room to find Pearce, still nude, his hands clasped behind his head, stretched out on the bed. Mark paused to let his gaze slide up the length of him— from his feet, up his strong, hairy legs, over his relaxed cock lolling across his thigh, along the flat line of his belly and swell of his chest, to his handsome face. He found it hard to believe sometimes that Aaron Pearce, FBI special agent and all-around cynical badass, was in love with him. And yet here lay the proof.

Mark's cock stirred at the sight of Pearce, and he glanced over at the clock, surprised to find it was six in the evening. He hated how fast time slipped away during vacations.

"Are you hungry?" Mark asked.

Pearce opened one eye, saw Mark was half-hard, and smirked. "You're ready to go again? What are you? Part rabbit?"

Mark grinned. "I might be."

"I need food first," Pearce said. "Unless you're trying to kill me?"

With a finger on his chin, Mark made an over-exaggerated expression of consideration. "Hmm."

Pearce got up and gave Mark's cock a tug as he strode past, headed for the bathroom. "Funny guy. I'll be right out."

Mark took a breath and let it out. Despite the sex and good-natured teasing, an underlying uneasiness had sprouted within him. He and Pearce had both been through a lot lately—Pearce on paid suspension and both of them involved in the shoot-out in the Speaker of the House's kitchen—so there were bound to be some lingering tensions. While their relationship felt strong, there had been subtle signs of strain. And, really, how could there not be? When Mark considered that he had lost his job at Filibuster Catering when the owner had been shot during the shoot-out, and he and Pearce had both been home in their small apartment, together, all day, every day. And now they shared a small hotel room, which could put a strain on any relationship—or reveal the cracks in their bond more easily.

He turned his thoughts away from such deep contemplation and to more immediate concerns, such as dinner. A good meal would help relax them both, and maybe they could talk a little more about things such as their life together at home without setting each other off.

Pearce emerged from the bathroom. He smacked Mark's bare ass in passing and sprawled out on the bed once again. Mark forced down a feeling of impatience – hadn't they just been talking about going to dinner? – and sat on the bed. He folded one leg so his thigh pressed against Pearce's hip.

"So, are you hungry?" he asked.

Pearce reached down to fondle Mark's cock. "You thinking of some red meat and cream sauce?"

Mark made a face. "I've heard it's a little tough."

"No, it's tender and relatable. Come on, try it."

"Well, maybe a taste." Mark bent over and put his lips around Pearce's cock. The salty flavor of Pearce's sweat burst across his tongue, and he blew a breath out his nostrils as he took him deep into his throat.

"Oh yeah, that's good," Pearce said, the timbre of his voice rumbling along Mark's spine and making his asshole twitch.

Mark sucked Pearce until he was fully erect, and then sat up, slowly stroking him as he said, "I need a good fuck."

Pearce smiled. "You've come to the right place. Grease it up, baby, and have a seat."

Mark chuckled as he leaned over to grab the lube off the night-stand. He drizzled some along Pearce's dick, spread it root to tip, and then straddled his hips. He lowered himself onto Pearce, pausing twice to rise before easing down again. Finally he sat fully impaled and clenched his muscles around the bare timber of his cock.

"Oh fuck." Pearce reached up to pull him down for a kiss. "I love this."

Mark lifted and lowered himself, gradually picking up speed, faster and faster, stroking his own cock as he moved. Pearce's dick stretched him, filled him, and poked stubbornly at the nugget of his prostate. They fit so well together, seemed to fill up each other's spaces so perfectly, Mark couldn't imagine being with anyone else.

"Yeah, you've got me close," Pearce said through a gasp. "Keep it up. Just like that."

"God, you feel so good inside me." Mark braced himself with one hand on Pearce's chest and felt his heart pound beneath his palm. He shifted position, and Pearce's cock hit him in just the right spot, immediately pushing him over the edge.

Mark's cock bucked in his hand, and a stream of cum splashed over Pearce's belly and chest. Pearce closed his eyes and let out a deep grunt as he lifted his hips to meet Mark on his downstroke, pushing his cock even deeper into him as he shot his load.

"Oh shit." Mark sat gasping on top of Pearce, still connected. "God, that was fucking hot."

Pearce caught his breath. "That flying fish really got to you."

Mark chuckled and eased off him. He walked on unsteady legs to the bathroom for a damp washcloth, which he used to clean himself up, then carried another one out to use on Pearce's cock and torso.

"Thanks," Pearce said. "Wow, great service at this hotel."

"We aim to please." Mark returned to the bathroom, saying over his shoulder, "I'm going to take a shower. Dinner after?"

"I've definitely worked up an appetite." Pearce rolled off the bed and followed Mark into the bathroom. "Can we share a shower to save some time?"

Mark nodded and started the water. "I guess so. As long as you don't get all handsy."

Pearce grinned and took hold of Mark's cock. "Like this?"

Mark smirked. "Yeah, like that."

Pearce reached lower and slipped his index finger into Mark's slick hole. "How about this?"

Mark braced himself against the wall as Pearce slowly slid his finger deeper. "Yeah, that could be called handsy."

"Maybe more fingery?"

The expression on Pearce's face was so intense and heated it made Mark shiver.

"I can feel my cum inside you," Pearce said in a low voice. He leaned in and kissed Mark softly on the mouth.

"Not that I'm not enjoying this," Mark said, "but I'm starving, and even though you're really turning me on, we'll have to table this for now." He stepped into the shower, feeling Pearce's finger drop out of him.

"Spoilsport," Pearce muttered as he stepped in behind him.

CHAPTER 6

The breeze off the ocean was warm and smelled of brine and fish and fading sunlight. Pearce couldn't recall a time when he'd been this relaxed and content. After their earlier friction, it felt good to just sit together and not talk. The afterglow of sex seemed to keep Mark and him in a cocoon apart from the other diners around them on the restaurant patio, and Pearce relished the moment.

As they ate, Pearce caught himself watching Mark's face as he stared across the beach and out to the sea. Pearce liked to think he knew Mark well by now and that Mark knew him also. They had been through some dangerous things together. Like the Kings of Rebellion plot back in Detroit, which had first brought them together, and the missing data discs in Washington, DC, which had made them realize they made a really good team.

Pearce figured they had earned these eight days in Barbados. He tried not to think about being on paid suspension from the FBI for having disobeyed orders and gone out into the field. Once they returned home, he'd have another five days off before he had to return to the office and his work, performing data searches for agents in the field.

Tension crackled up the back of his neck, and Pearce forced thoughts of DC and the FBI out of his mind and went back to eating. The sea bass was fresh and the red-skin potatoes perfectly seasoned. He needed to focus on the moment and enjoy being here, with Mark, full and content in the warm evening on the beach.

He looked across the table in time to catch a shadow of a frown cross Mark's face. At first, Pearce wondered if it hadn't been caused by the flickering candle between them. But then he saw it again, along with Mark's wrinkled brow and slightly narrowed eyes. Something was on Mark's mind, something troubling, and Pearce hoped it wasn't something he had done or said earlier that Mark hadn't been able to let go.

Then again, maybe Mark was thinking about something completely different. His every single thought couldn't be about Pearce or their relationship. He just needed to let Mark have some space and his own thoughts and they would be okay. Wouldn't they?

A tiny, niggling doubt formed in the back of his mind. Was he back to his old tricks now, trying to find something that annoyed him about Mark? Was this some kind of relationship self-sabotage ploy he was pulling? He had thought he'd gotten through that phase with Mark, but maybe he'd just managed to put it into remission for a while.

Either way, from the expression on his face, Mark's thoughts had taken a darker turn, and Pearce wondered where they had gone.

"You okay over there?"

"Huh?" Mark's gaze was distant behind the lenses of his glasses. "Oh. Yeah. I'm good. Just taking it all in."

"Yeah? Not thinking about anything in particular?" Pearce speared a bite of fish and looked around for the waiter to order another beer.

Mark shrugged. "Well, maybe. I was thinking about that girl at the bar." He gave Pearce a small smile. "Can't get anything past Special Agent Pearce, can I?"

"Sooner you realize that and just say stuff up front, the easier it'll be for both of us," Pearce said.

"Yeah, yeah." Mark shook his head. "I keep thinking about how she seemed to be trying to talk to me as we were leaving. I wonder what she was saying?"

Pearce cocked his head. "She spoke to you?"

Mark widened his eyes. "Didn't I tell you?"

"No. How did she speak to you? I was right there, and I didn't hear her."

"Well, she didn't actually say anything, not with that guy right there. But she mouthed something to me."

Pearce took a breath and let it out. "She mouthed something?"

Mark shut down immediately. Pearce could see it in his expression, and wanted to kick himself for the tone he'd taken.

"I knew you wouldn't believe me," Mark said.

Pearce shook his head. He was on vacation, damn it, and he didn't want to get involved in whatever was going on in that run-down bar with that girl who had made bad decisions all her life. But he knew Mark wouldn't be able to relax for the remainder of their time on the island if they didn't do something. And besides, now that Mark had brought her up again, Pearce himself was starting to wonder if the girl might be in trouble.

"Do you want to go back there tomorrow?" Pearce tried this time to cover up the minor aggravation he was feeling.

Mark seemed surprised. "You'd do that with me?"

"If it will help you relax and enjoy the rest of our trip, I would do that with you."

"Well, yeah, that would be great, actually. Just to see, you know?"

Pearce put his fork down and wiped his mouth. "One condition."

Mark sat back. "There's a condition?"

Pearce nodded. "If we go to that bar and she's not there, do you think you can let it go and enjoy the rest of the trip?"

A long moment of silence passed, during which time Pearce felt a tremor of nerves as he waited for Mark's response. Had he over-stepped a boundary by putting a condition on his willingness to go to the bar with Mark?

Mark sighed and slouched in his chair. "Yeah, okay. I see your point."

Pearce raised his eyebrows. "Do you really, or are you just saying that?"

Mark glared at him. "I see it, smart-ass. I guess that girl's resem-blance to Summer from my high school kind of set a tone for the day." He made a face. "Sorry."

Leaning in over the table, Pearce lowered his voice and said, "We're both a little edgy, I think, right? We've been through a lot in the last few months, but we did it together. We just need to focus on that, and we'll be fine." He sat back, feeling pretty proud of himself for what he'd just said. Then he checked to make sure no one was close enough before leaning in again to say, "Besides, we had some pretty fucking hot sex when we got back to the room."

Mark's blush was answer enough for Pearce, and he sat back again, content and more relaxed.

THE RIDE to the Bridgetown Bar the next day took less time now that they had a destination. It was a little past noon when Pearce followed Mark's scooter in to the white-gravel lot. The Flying Fish Eatery was open, and two couples were approaching the door, laughing and talking. On the other side of the parking lot, the porch of the Bridgetown Bar was empty. Pearce was glad not to see the guy from the day sitting there like some kind of guard.

"Want to check the place out?" Pearce asked.

Mark nodded and Pearce followed him across the gravel lot, up the faded wooden steps and through the screen door.

The patrons were mostly men, all of them Bajan, and every conversation stopped as each patron turned toward them. It had all the trappings of a cliché-riddled movie, only this was real life and the moment raised the hairs on the back of Pearce's neck. A small bar sat in the back corner, big enough for only four men to sit along the front. The bartender was a heavyset man with small, dark eyes and a hard expression. A wave of distrust seemed to roll toward them from the crowd as a ceiling fan directly above Pearce stirred the grease-tinged air and sent a chill along the sweat-damp skin over his spine.

An older waitress pushed through a swinging door at the back of the bar, hands clutching a large tray loaded with plates and glasses of beer. She saw them hovering by the door and stopped in surprise.

"You lost?" she asked, and loud, unsettling laughter filled the bar.

"No, just wanted to check the place out," Pearce said. "Heard a lot about it."

The waitress stared at them a moment, then lifted her chin to gesture to an empty table in the corner. "Open table there."

As they sat, Pearce sensed Mark's mood fall. He knew Mark had been hoping to see the girl again, maybe get a chance to talk with her and make sure she wasn't being held against her will. Pearce knew about the dangers of girls being abducted and sold into sex slavery. He'd read reports about it back at the FBI, surprised to find that it was a more common crime in the United States than most people realized. It recurred frighteningly often in certain countries, where young girls—many times Americans—were lured away from their friends with the promise of alcohol or drugs. Once separated, they were subdued and turned over to brutal men who in turn sold them to buyers to do with as they pleased. And then the girls were never heard from again.

When Pearce thought about that kind of life, a cold, dark pit opened inside him. How did a family cope with never knowing what happened to their loved one?

"She's not here," Mark said.

"Nope, I don't see her." Pearce scanned the faces of the people at the tables, but none of them met his gaze, and he figured they wouldn't answer any questions if he tried to ask anyway. "Want to ask the bartender?"

Mark nodded. "Yeah. Let's do that at least."

Pearce got up and led the way to the bar. The big man watched their approach with suspicion, his large hands spread on the top of the small bar. Pearce wedged himself in between two men sitting on stools and nodded as he met the bartender's eyes.

"Drinks?" the man asked, his voice deep and rumbling.

"Bottled beer," Pearce said.

"Same," Mark added from behind him.

The bartender fetched a couple of bottles from a glass-fronted refrigerator and popped off the caps. When Pearce lifted the bottle for a drink, it felt cool but not cold, and he tried unsuccessfully not to flinch when he took the first swig.

"Americans?" the burly man asked in a tone more accusatory than inquisitive.

Pearce flashed a smile. "That obvious, huh?"

The man shrugged his broad shoulders and used a damp towel to wipe the already-clean surface before him.

"There were a few girls here yesterday," Mark said. "Standing out on the porch."

The bartender glared at Mark over Pearce's shoulder. "Get a lot of people in here. Don't know 'em."

Pearce jumped in before Mark could continue. "Sure you don't know 'em? Three girls, all white, one with long blonde hair. My friend here thinks he might know her from back home, wanted to talk with her a bit."

A shrug was his only response, and Pearce sighed and pulled out his wallet. He extracted a fifty-dollar bill and slid it across the bar. "Sure you don't remember them?"

The bartender pocketed the fifty and stared Pearce in the eye. "Nope. Don't know 'em. Like I said, we get a lot of people in here."

Mark made a sound of disgust as Pearce surveyed the half-empty bar. "Yeah, I can see that." He drank half his beer and nodded down to the pocket where his money had disappeared. "Take the cost of our beers out of your tip."

That got a hint of a smile, and Pearce turned away to cross the room and return to the corner table. Mark sat beside him, both of them putting their backs to the wall. Pearce kept his eye on the men at the bar as Mark bounced his leg beneath the table.

"Fifty bucks down the shitter," Pearce grumbled.

"I can't believe you tried to bribe him," Mark whispered.

Pearce slid him a cool look from the corner of his eye. "What did you want me to do?"

Mark shrugged. "I don't know. I guess I didn't think about how we'd get information out of someone. I was hoping they'd just be here again."

"Well, keep hoping. That was part of our souvenir budget. Good thing you've already bought those flip-flops."

Mark snorted. "Damn cheap things."

"You fixed them," Pearce muttered.

"Damn right I did," Mark replied with a firm nod. "I'm unemployed. I gotta make things last. I paid for them, and I'm going to rig them up any way I need to."

"Classy."

"Nothing but the best for me," Mark said, and his smile got Pearce to smile as well. "Bread-bag tags and cheap rubber flip-flops."

The door to the kitchen swung open, and the waitress ambled out. She saw them sitting at the table with their beers and walked up, pulling out a pad of paper. "You want food with those beers?"

"I think we're set for now," Pearce said. "But we were wondering about a group of women we saw here yesterday. Do you know them?"

She stared at Pearce a long moment, her lips pressed tight together. "Women? What did they look like? We get a lot of people in here."

"So we keep hearing," Pearce said.

"They were white girls," Mark spoke up. "Three of them. One had long blonde hair and was very pale. They were standing out on the porch yesterday afternoon."

The waitress looked between them in silence, then sighed and dropped her order pad back into the pocket of her apron. In a tired, used-up voice, she said, "If they don't come inside the bar, I don't see 'em. And I don't handle orders at the bar. That's Abraham's area."

"Yeah, we've already talked with *Abraham*, and he didn't seem to remember them either," Pearce said. "Sure you don't know the girls? My friend here thinks he might know one of them from back home."

The waitress waved his words away. "Oh, you know, there a lot of people in this world. Everyone got a double, they say. Probably you just saw your friend's double." She turned and walked away.

Mark sighed. "Well, they both shut us down pretty fast."

"Not surprising." Pearce finished his beer. "I think it's time to go, don't you?"

"Yeah, it is." Mark drained his beer.

Pearce pushed back his chair and stood, nodding across the room to Abraham the bartender, who simply stared back. Pearce led the way out of the bar and across the gravel lot to their scooters.

"I'm surprised the waitress didn't help us out more," Mark said, straddling his scooter. "You'd think she'd want to help other women. What do you think was going on with those girls?"

"Could be a lot of things," Pearce replied. "Drug dealers with prostitutes, a group of low-income girls who just hang out there trying to land a sugar daddy, or the girls could be held against their will."

Mark looked down at the dials of his scooter. "I wish we'd been able to tell which one of those it was."

"I know. But they're gone, right? We came back today to check for them, and they aren't here. If we go to the police, we could make a report, but there's no evidence of anything, and we've got no names and no other details. We've got no more information, and I'm out fifty bucks. Can you let it go?"

Mark surveyed the bar, his leg bouncing, and then turned back to Pearce. "Yeah. You're right. Let's go back to the hotel."

"Okay. Let's go." Pearce started the scooter and waited for Mark to lead the way. With a final glance at the Bridgetown Bar, Pearce pulled out after Mark and followed him down the road.

CHAPTER 7

The next morning, Mark stepped through the door of the hotel's dining area and smiled. The breakfast buffet attracted the usual suspects on an island vacation. A few pairs of newlyweds huddling at out-of-the-way tables to stare at each other over their food. Some older couples lingering over coffee and a newspaper, trading sections and commenting now and then on other guests or a bit of local news. And families, the parents—outnumbered by children—trying to get each of their brood to eat in the midst of planning the day of sightseeing or playing on the beach.

He made his way through the tables and stood in line for the omelet station, watching with detached interest as the chef, Salvador, prepared omelets for a couple in front of him. When Salvador had sent the man and woman on their way with a smile, he turned to Mark, and his smile widened.

"Mark! How are you this morning?" Salvador broke three eggs into a small silver bowl and began to whisk them together. "The usual order?"

Mark nodded and stifled a yawn. "Sorry, Salvador. Guess I was up too late last night."

"Enjoying the beach at night?" Salvador waggled his eyebrows as he added diced ham, chopped peppers, and artichoke hearts to the bowl.

"Very much," Mark replied.

"Where is your friend? Aaron?"

"Back in the room, still asleep." Mark noticed there was no one else standing near them, and he leaned in closer. "Salvador, how long have you lived in Barbados?"

"All my life, my friend," Salvador replied as he poured the egg mixture into a small pan and set it on a hot plate.

"Do you know Bridgetown very well?"

"I was born in Bridgetown and live there to this day. What can I help you find in our beautiful city?"

Mark smiled; it was difficult not to with Salvador's bright patter and broad grin. "Well, actually, I was wondering if you knew of a place called the Bridgetown Bar? It's a bit off the main routes. Shares a parking lot with the Flying Fish Eatery?"

Salvador looked at him for a long moment, the intensity of his gaze not matching the smile he kept pasted on his face. "The Bridgetown Bar, you say?"

"Yeah, Bridgetown Bar."

"Why do you ask that, friend?"

Mark leaned back and tried to appear more casual, but Salvador's reaction had him on alert now. He thought he should proceed with a bit more caution. It was a small island, after all. Perhaps Salvador and the bartender were related. "Oh, no reason. We just happened on it the other day. We ate at the Flying Fish Eatery and saw it as we were leaving. Thought it seemed like a good local place for a beer. I wondered what you thought of it. That's all."

"I know the owner, Abraham." Salvador flipped Mark's omelet and lifted his gaze quickly before looking back down at the pan. "It's more a place for locals, not really meant for tourists."

"Well, like I said, we wanted more of a local experience."

"If you like, I can suggest some better places for you and your friend to visit." Salvador slid Mark's omelet onto a plate and handed it over. "Places with much better food and drinks than the Bridgetown Bar, of that I can assure you."

"You know, I think we've decided to spend a few days here at the beach just relaxing." Mark lifted his plate. "Thanks for the omelet."

"Enjoy your day on the beach, Mark," Salvador said as Mark turned away. "Don't stay out so long you get burned."

Mark made his way to a table set away from the chaos of the families and grinned to himself when he discovered he had selected the newlywed section. Well, that was kind of how he had hoped this trip would feel to him, to them both. He had discovered a whole new side of Pearce on this vacation. A romantic side, more open and loving. But they'd also dealt with a lot of minor misunderstandings that had derailed some of those more tender moments. He would have been an idiot to expect a smooth vacation experience; he had pushed Pearce into coming here, after all. But Mark wasn't sure if these momentary tensions happened in every relationship. He'd been with Eric back in Detroit and a couple of men before that, but those dalliances never lasted more than six weeks. Did the tiny disagreements seem bigger because the emotions ran deeper between him and Pearce? Or were they just two stubborn, mismatched men who liked sex?

As he unrolled his utensils from the cloth napkin, Mark sighed and shook his head. He had never expected to get this close to someone. Based on his past relationships, he'd thought he would simply tolerate someone. But now here was Aaron Pearce—complicated, tough, reluctantly romantic, and about as far outside of Mark's expectations for the man he'd end up with as one could get.

Damn it. Couldn't one thing just be easy?

Another newlywed couple entered the dining room, the bride

giggling at something her husband was whispering in her ear. The woman had long blonde hair, and Mark's thoughts shifted to the girl at the Bridgetown Bar. He could still picture her haunted eyes, lank hair, and pale face. He thought about the way she had scratched at her arms and realized it reminded him of the squirrels he had seen back home in Detroit who had caught mange, how they scratched and scratched at themselves until their fur came off in patches. He wondered what this girl's name was, how she had come to be here, in Barbados, and in the company of that man on the porch. But most of all he wondered what she had tried to say to him as he and Pearce had been leaving the bar.

"Hey, there."

Mark jumped and looked up to find Pearce standing beside the table. His hair was wet from the shower, and he smelled of body-wash and shampoo.

"Jeez, you scared me." Mark dropped his gaze to his plate, away from Pearce's stare.

"You okay?"

Mark nodded, glancing away again. "Yeah. Just kind of lost in my own little world here. That's all." A hot flash of guilt heated his face, and he didn't want Pearce to see him blushing. How could he sit here and act so innocent, as if he hadn't been questioning the strength of their relationship? And to top it off, he'd been caught thinking about that girl at the bar after telling Pearce he would let his concerns about her go and enjoy the rest of their vacation.

Pearce studied him a moment before setting his sunglasses on the table. "Okay. I'm going to make Salvador earn his keep with one hell of an omelet order. Need anything from the buffet while I'm up there?"

"Nope, all set. Thanks." Mark watched Pearce's back as he moved through the dining room. Every woman turned as he walked past—and a couple of the men as well—and Mark smirked down at his omelet. He pushed his contemplation of their misunderstandings and his thoughts of the girl at the bar aside and focused on his life with Pearce. He really enjoyed knowing the terrain of Pearce's body so well, all his sensitive spots and the marks his life had left on him, the scars and wrinkles. Mark also appreciated Pearce's humor—dark, cutting, and wicked—and his insight into human behavior, frustrating as it was to try and hide something from him. Like today, for instance, when Pearce had caught him deep in thought here at the table. Pearce would know, of course, that Mark had been thinking about the girl at the bar. It was in Pearce's DNA to know when people were lying or only telling part of the truth. That was what made him such a good special agent—and one hell of a difficult man to live with sometimes.

When Pearce returned to the table with his overstuffed omelet, he sat across from Mark and looked from the circus of the family tables to the quiet newlywed tables nearby. "Guess we more closely match up with the newlyweds?"

Mark nodded and grinned. "Felt like it yesterday."

Pearce flashed him a promising smile. "It could again today too."

"I like the sound of that," Mark said and finished his omelet.

He pushed aside his plate, and as Pearce dug into his own breakfast, Mark looked around the room. His gaze came to rest on the pretty blonde woman sitting with her handsome new husband a few tables away. She tipped back her head as she laughed at something her husband said, the sound was bright as it drifted through the sunlit dining room. She was a complete contrast to the blonde girl at the Bridgetown Bar, and an ugly sense of dread gnawed steadily into his gut. He knew that girl was in trouble; he *knew* it. But what could he do about it? Would no one else see her situation clearly? Would no one else take a stand to help her? What could he, a visitor in a foreign country, do for her?

He looked across the table and found Pearce staring at him.

"What's on your mind?"

"What?"

"You were deep in thought," Pearce explained. "I was just wondering what you were thinking about."

"Oh. Nothing. Just, you know, thinking. That's all."

"You said you could let it go."

Anger flared up within Mark, sudden and awful, a flash fire of guilt and frustration and helplessness that overrode his logic and reasoning. Yes, he had told Pearce he would stop obsessing about the girl from the bar, but how would that make things better? She was just a young girl, no more than twenty-one, and she could very well be in danger. If she were one of his sisters, or his friend, or even his daughter, he'd want a stranger who noticed her to step in and help her if she needed it.

"Well, damn it, I'm trying, okay?" Mark snapped, his voice louder than he had intended. A wicked sense of shame swamped him, but it only served to fuel his guilty feelings and, with them, his anger at Pearce. How could Pearce not have seen what Mark had seen? How could he turn a blind eye to a young girl in trouble? He was a public servant, sworn to uphold the law, and even though they were not in their homeland, some things should not be turned away from. Some things, no matter how ugly and how difficult to prove, must have a light shined on them.

"Keep your voice down," Pearce said, his tone calm and even, but the anger in his stare hot and evident. "I asked you a simple question."

Mark leaned in over the table, his forearm landing on the handle of his fork and sending it clattering across the plate, attracting even more attention, but he was beyond caring about that now. Pearce had lanced Mark's scabbed-over anxiety, and no amount of rational discussion would be able to stem the flow of it. "And I'm giving you a simple response. I have tried to stop thinking about her, but goddamn it, I know something's wrong. And the fact that we're not doing more to try to help her out is killing me, okay? Are you really, truly that callous now? Is this what your job has done to you?"

"Lower. Your. Voice. We'll discuss this in the room."

Mark pushed back his chair and rose to his feet. He wasn't thinking clearly; he knew it, and he just wanted to get out. Get out of the hotel and get away from Pearce for a little while. He walked quickly through the dining room, not stopping when he heard Pearce's sharp-toned, "Mark!" and ignoring the curious looks he received.

He knew he'd overreacted, but there was no going back and fixing it now. He needed to clear his head and get some perspective, try to get past the memory of Summer Barrington's disappearance so many years ago. How could he let the same thing happen to another family somewhere? He had seen Summer's mother in the grocery store once during those hot summer months before his junior year. The woman's hollow-eyed stare as she led Summer's younger sister and brother through the aisles had chilled him then and haunted him to this day, calling to him to somehow, someway, help this other girl. Bring some closure to her family, wherever they might be now.

The sunlight stung his eyes as he pushed out of the lobby doors, and he paused to put his hand up at his brow to shade his face. Seabirds circled the beach, their calls raucous and piercing, seeming to drill right into the center of Mark's head and tap at the seed of guilt there—guilt from his overreaction with Pearce and guilt from not doing more to help the blonde girl at the bar. The white sand shimmered in the sun's heat, hotel guests just starting to stake out their spots, and Mark's anxiety amped up a few more notches. He didn't want to be in a crowd of people, and he didn't want to go back to the room, where Pearce would storm in, corner him, and force him into an argument Mark knew he would lose.

He turned and walked as quickly as he was able to in his flip-flops—his cheap-ass flip-flops he'd patched like a beggar because he had no job waiting for him back home. More guilt. More anxiety. His body felt like it was filled with tension and his head like it was about to pop off from the pressure inside him. He needed to cool down, feel the wind on his face. After rounding the freshwater pool deck, Mark approached the scooter rental booth. The attendant, a young kid with a quick smile, recognized him and reached over to nab a set of keys from the board. "You going for another ride today?"

Mark smiled as best he could and reached out for the keys. "Yeah. Seems like a good day for a ride."

"Your friend going too?"

Mark shook his head as he signed the waiver and added his room number for the billing. "Not this time. He's got other plans today."

"Well, enjoy, my friend," the kid said and waved to the scooters lined up along the sidewalk. "I gave you the same scooter you had before, waiting right where you left her. All gassed up and ready to go."

"Thanks. I'll see you later." Mark waved and then moved up to the scooter. He started the small engine, set his feet into the footwells, and after drawing in a breath, he puttered out onto the road.

THE WORDS STAMPEDED through Pearce's mind as he ate his omelet, the taste not even registering. Where the hell had this argument come from? He tried to trace Mark's blowup back to where it had started, the need to understand gnawing at him. This was what made him a good agent but an annoying boyfriend, or so he'd been told.

He chewed his food and glared at the newlyweds who sat at tables around him, giggling and blushing once again now that the show between him and Mark had ended. He forced down his mouthful of food and sighed as he turned away from them. Things between him and Mark had been going so well; he really wanted to figure out what he'd done so he could avoid these kinds of scenes in the future.

He bit into a piece of toast and stared at a painting directly across from him. It was a watercolor of men on a fishing boat, pulling in a net of thrashing, jumping fish. Pearce could sympathize with the fish. He felt like he was being dragged into a place with no way to breathe, and it happened suddenly and, it felt, very violently. Was this what being in a relationship was supposed to feel like?

He really didn't have a lot of experience with which to compare notes. His only other relationship that had lasted longer than three dates had been Robert Morgan, and that had turned out pretty fucking bad. Not only had Morgan degraded Pearce when they'd been together at the academy, but the man had become even more twisted after they'd broken up—if one could call becoming a mole for a terrorist group and plotting to murder hundreds of innocent civilians twisted.

Pearce rotated his right arm, stretching the muscle so recently healed after Morgan had stabbed him in the shoulder. If it hadn't been for Mark saving him, Pearce would have died in that abandoned house in Detroit.

Mark.

Damn it, why did his every thought have to lead right back to Mark? What the fuck had happened to the tough-ass special-agent persona he had used to keep everyone at a distance? Dead and gone, so it would appear. The assignment to protect Mark had ruined him.

Or made him complete. It seemed to change depending on the day —and each of their moods.

Pearce cocked his head as he studied the fish in the painting. That was an interesting thought. Not just Mark's mood, but his as well. Maybe he was more to blame for these conversations that degenerated into minor tantrums than he liked to admit.

He tossed the last crust of bread onto his plate and let his gaze fall on the tray of dirty dishes Mark had left behind. Only half the omelet had been eaten and none of the toast. The way Mark liked to eat breakfast, he would have started on the toast in the next few minutes if he had stayed. He liked to eat half the main dish first, take a break from that to eat half his toast, and then finish the main dish before ending with whatever toast he was hungry for.

"You're so whipped," Pearce mumbled to himself and shook his head. Only a stalker would know detailed shit like that. Or someone who was in love.

"All finished here?"

Pearce jerked his head up to find a young busboy standing by the table. The kid's gloved hand was poised near the edge of Mark's tray as he looked at Pearce, waiting for permission to remove it. Pearce nodded and wiped his mouth with his napkin before sitting back.

"You can take both trays," he said. "Thanks."

The kid nodded and smiled as he efficiently whisked away the trays. "Good day to you, sir."

"Yeah, you too." Pearce looked at the painting another moment, shifting his perspective from that of the fish to that of the fisherman. Maybe he had just hooked a big marlin—a real keeper—and he was still fighting it, working hard to guess when it was going to dive and jump and lurch left and right as he reeled it in.

And maybe he should stop seeing his relationship as an allegory to a goddamn painting in a resort dining room and just get up off his ass to go find Mark.

"Damn it." Pearce pushed back from the table and got to his feet, then snatched up his sunglasses and headed for the door.

"Have a good day!" someone called, and Pearce turned to see the omelet chef, the young kid Mark had befriended, waving to him. The kid was cleaning up his station as he got ready to leave for the day.

Pearce lifted his hand in a wave and walked out into the lobby. He crossed to the door that opened toward the beach and pushed out into the bright sunlight. Another gorgeous day here in Barbados. As he made his way along the concrete path toward the fresh-water pool and the sandy beach beyond, he wondered if the islanders took these kinds of days for granted. From what he'd seen on the weather channel, the average temperature was eighty-five with a breeze off the ocean. Would it be worth the threat of hurricanes to live here? Run a tiny bar, maybe? Or a souvenir shop?

People were setting up on the beach, laying claim to prime sunning spots and umbrellas. Pearce really wanted to spend at least one day relaxing on the beach. No running around seeing sites, no timetables, no thoughts other than if he was wearing enough sunscreen and whether he wanted a mango or banana daiquiri for his next drink.

But first he needed to find Mark and put things right. Mark cared about others; Pearce knew that, but his concern about a complete stranger more than demonstrated it. Instead of being angry with Mark for trying to help someone who might be in trouble, Pearce should encourage and, damn it, work with him. Mark might have overreacted, but Pearce knew he had as well.

Would it get any easier? He blew out a breath, knowing that it would get easier, and a lot better. He also knew that Mark was worth the work. He just needed to make sure Mark was aware that Pearce knew it.

He walked along the beach, swiveling his head back and forth, checking for Mark on each lounger and beneath each umbrella. He was nowhere to be found. That didn't really surprise Pearce, though. He figured Mark needed some time to blow off steam; he liked to be on his own when he was feeling as agitated as Mark had acted. Which meant he was probably up in the room, pacing and grumbling to himself.

Pearce had slipped the sunscreen into the pocket of his shorts, so he decided the best thing he could do was let Mark stew in the room for a bit. His search shifted from looking for Mark to finding a lounger before all the good spots were taken. Vacation priorities were reinstated, and the feeling of anxiety that had wound tightly into his chest like a cold, sharp corkscrew eased back a bit. Not much, but enough to allow him to weigh his options for sunbathing spots.

After grabbing a couple of towels from the shelves near the pool, Pearce tromped through the steadily warming sand to a lounger set off from the rest. Perfect for a lone-wolf FBI special agent such as himself. He spread out a towel, stripped off his shirt, and sat down. As he worked sunscreen into his skin, he thought about the complete disconnect this trip to Barbados meant. They were on a budget, and that meant no international mobile phone service. Without the ability to text or make quick calls, he and Mark really needed to be more vigilant about telling each other where they were going and for how long.

A quiet sense of uneasiness twisted through his gut, and with a frown, he looked toward the hotel. Counting up the windows to the fifth floor, he tried to pick out the one to their room but was unable to get it right. He considered abandoning his lounger and heading up to the room to check on Mark but then let the thought go. He'd give Mark his space.

So decided, Pearce stretched out along the lounger, took a deep breath of clean, ocean-scented air, and closed his eyes.

CHAPTER 8

Mark knew what he was doing wasn't smart, but it didn't seem to matter. It was the uncertainty of the situation, the "unknowing," that stuck in his mind like a sliver. And the only way to get rid of a sliver that got in this deep was to dig it out, and that was what he was doing now.

He rounded a bend in the road and saw the buildings of Bridgetown up ahead. He was headed right back to the Bridgetown Bar, and though he was alone and it might be dangerous, he had to try to find out more about that girl.

He thought about the way he'd acted with Pearce in the dining hall and felt a sunburst of shame. Why had he been so quick to lose his temper when Pearce had brought it up? Because somewhere inside himself, he knew Pearce was right. He should let this go; he was on a losing mission. He was a foreigner on this island, here for a limited time and with no power or recourse.

But he couldn't just let this girl continue to suffer if she was in trouble. He had to know for sure; he had to check at least one more time. If he was stonewalled this time, Mark would go to the police and file a report, have them take over, and then he'd let it go, once and for all. He'd have to; there would be nothing more he could do. He would tell the police his suspicions and go back to the hotel, find Pearce where he would be sunning himself on the beach, and apologize. Maybe lure him up to the room for some hot, sweaty makeup sex before they returned to the beach to relax together.

Emboldened by his vision of being back with Pearce soon, Mark pulled in to the Bridgetown Bar parking lot, the white gravel crunching quietly beneath the tires, and killed the motor of his scooter. The porch of the bar was empty, but he heard the muted sound of conversations drifting out the screen door and a deep, heavy, male laugh that had a hard edge to it. It sent a shudder through Mark, and he remained on the seat of the scooter a moment, studying the bar and trying to decide on a course of action. If he simply walked in and started asking questions, he was sure he'd be shut down right away.

A sound from the rear of the building caught his attention, and Mark turned to look in that direction. A cement path, cracked, pitted, and dotted with weeds, led from the parking lot to the back corner of the bar. Another sound, this one louder, got him off the scooter, and he stood alongside it, one hand resting on a handlebar as if it were a touchstone of safety. Had that been the sound of someone whimpering? Someone in pain?

He acted on instinct. Leaving the scooter, he crossed the parking lot. The gravel ground loudly as he moved to the narrow cement path that circled the bar. He paused to remove his flip-flops and, holding them in one hand, continued barefoot along the path to the rear corner of the building. More sounds—moaning and whimpering, it sounded like. Could someone be having sex behind the bar? If that was the case, Mark didn't want to intrude.

Turning away from the corner, Mark took one step back along the path but then heard the unmistakable sound of a slap and a woman crying out in surprise and pain. He reacted without thought. He tightened his grip on his flip-flops and stepped around the corner. A group of Bajan men stood at the back of a late-model minivan, the rear doors flung open and the windows tinted dark enough to prevent anyone from seeing inside. On the ground at their feet was the young blonde girl he'd seen on the porch, her legs curled under her and a hand touching her cheek that Mark could see was red from the slap she'd been given. As Mark watched, one of the men tucked himself back inside his pants and zipped up.

"Hey!" Mark said before he could think about what he was doing.

The men looked at him, startled, and the blonde girl turned to reach out to him.

"Please," she said.

"Shut up, bitch," barked one of the men. He pulled back his foot to deliver a kick, and white-hot anger burned through Mark.

"Stop it!" Mark shouted and then took a step back as the man who had been zipping his pants approached.

Mark turned to look for help from someone—anyone—but stopped in his tracks, the flip-flops falling from his hands as he found another man had come up behind him. He felt the hard poke of a gun in his ribs, and a cold flood of terror followed as he looked up into the angry face of Abraham the bartender.

"You kind of nosy for a tourist," Abraham rumbled down at him.

Strong hands gripped Mark's arms and turned him around, then pushed him toward the van. Rocks bit into the soles of his bare feet as he stumbled up against the vehicle. The blonde girl had gotten to her feet and leaned against the van beside him.

"You okay?" Mark asked.

"Shut the fuck up," one of the men shouted. "You don't talk to the merchandise."

Mark stepped toward the man, anger and terror swirling

together within him. He clenched his fists and glared at him. "People are not merchandise."

"Kill him?" a man asked, his voice calm and quiet, and Mark saw it was the man who had been raping the girl. There was no emotion in the man's eyes, no sense of empathy or compassion as he lifted his arm to aim a gun at Mark's head.

Mark felt truly afraid for his life. After all he'd been through, he was going to die here in Barbados, behind this bar, and his body would be dumped in the sea. He would never see Pearce again, and Pearce would never find him, never know what happened to him, and a terrible, aching pit of regret opened within him. He had been so very stupid to come back to this bar alone.

"Wait," the bartender said, holding up a hand. The rapist lowered the gun but kept his icy gaze fixed on Mark.

"What you doing, Abraham?" one of the other men asked. "Kill him!"

Abraham took two steps closer as a high-pitched buzz of panic started in Mark's head. His breath came in short pants, and the ground felt as if it shifted continually beneath him. He tightened his jaw and made himself look up into Abraham's dark eyes.

"I know someone who might pay a high price for a blond American man," Abraham said.

"You selling bullas now?" asked one of the men.

Abraham smiled coldly down at Mark and said, "I'd sell anything for a good profit. Including your bulla hole."

Laughter all around. Behind Mark, the blonde girl vomited loudly onto the gravel. The men laughed as Mark stood shivering before them. A touch on his arm made him jump, and he turned to see the blonde girl standing just behind his shoulder. She clung to him, her fingers chilled, her grip tight, and her breath horrendous as she said repeatedly, "Help me. Help me. Help me."

Abraham chuckled, the sound like a deep, wet gurgle. "Oh,

pretty thing. He just might be in more trouble than you." Abraham looked at the rapist standing behind him, the gun still in his hand. "Bring both of them in the van. We need to get out of here before more people show up."

The rapist nodded and approached Mark and the girl. Mark raised his hands to try to defend himself, and the girl holding on to him looked up, saw the man coming, and let out a scream that made Mark flinch and turn away. He felt a blow on the back of his head, and then darkness rushed up to take him.

A SCREAM WOKE Pearce from his doze. He sat up and looked around, finding his place in the world and then the situations of those around him.

He was in Barbados, on the beach, alone but surrounded by other hotel guests. He could see no threat—the scream had been from one of the newlyweds horsing around in the water.

He noticed next how warm he felt. How long had he been baking there in the sun? He turned right and then left, felt his spine crackle all the way up, and sighed. Keeping his sunglasses on, he pushed to his feet and quick-stepped over the hot sand to the water. The gentle chill nipped into his skin, cooling him down and making him shiver. He turned to face the beach and lowered himself into the water, letting out a quiet breath of relief as the cool water washed over his brown, sweaty skin. Mark would have watched the time for him if he'd been around.

As Pearce floated in the water, letting the gentle waves wash over him and push him toward shore, he scanned the beach. Maybe Mark had come down after Pearce had dozed off and just not seen him. He squinted and checked every group, even those who appeared to be together, just in case Mark had befriended someone. But there was no sign of him.

His feet touched the sandy bottom, and Pearce rose out of the water, then crossed the beach to his lounger. He dried off quickly, scooped up his shirt and the sunscreen, and started toward the hotel. The room key card was still in the button-flap pocket of his shorts, and he pulled it out as he entered the lobby and crossed to the elevator.

The hallway on their floor was empty—even the maids had finished their rounds—and he was surprised to find he was trembling. His fingers felt cold as he stopped in front of their room and fumbled with the key card. The lock released, and he pushed inside, Mark's name dying on his lips when he found the room was empty. The bed was made up, and fresh towels hung in the bathroom, but other than that there was no sign anyone had been in the room since that morning.

Pearce thought Mark might have at least left him a note telling him where he'd gone, but no. He opened drawers and was relieved to find Mark's clothes still folded neatly alongside his. At least he hadn't been angry enough to just pack up and leave altogether. Mark had to be somewhere around the hotel. Maybe he had gone for a walk along the beach and hadn't realized how far he'd traveled until he had to start back?

A ball of sweat rolled into his left eye. Pearce cursed as he rubbed it and then cursed louder when he got sunscreen in his eye. Even though he wanted to go out and look for Mark, he needed a shower first. He stepped out of his flip-flops and headed for the bathroom.

It took longer than he had hoped to scrub himself clean, and in his rush he almost slipped and fell twice in the oil slick of lotion at the bottom of the tub. Finally he walked out of the bathroom with a towel around his waist and drops of water on his shoulders and chest. He caught a glimpse of his reflection in the mirror and was startled at how much he had tanned. A glance at the clock increased his pulse as he discovered it was already late afternoon. Mark had been gone for too long without checking in. Pearce was now officially concerned as he abandoned the towel and hurriedly pulled on some clothes.

The elevator ride to the first floor seemed to take an eternity. He stepped out into the lobby and stopped to look around, his hope that he would find Mark simply sitting in a chair, reading a book or newspaper, fading as he recognized no one. Pearce crossed to the desk and waited as the clerk behind the counter, a pretty, young woman, went over a map with another guest. He tried not to become impatient, but it grew increasingly difficult as the man in front of him asked question after insipid question. At last the man thanked the clerk and walked off, allowing Pearce to step up.

"May I help you, sir?" the woman asked.

"Hi, yeah," Pearce said, then stopped, unsure of what he wanted to ask. Mark was gone, but Pearce had no idea where. What should he ask? Had she seen Mark? Would she know who Mark was even if she had seen him? And what if Mark had taken a cab to town and was just shopping? Without their cell phones, they needed to rely on notes or telling each other where they were going.

"Sir?" The woman frowned at him. "Are you all right?"

"My boyfr... Well, see, I haven't seen my, um, my travel companion for a few hours now, and I was wondering if you might have seen him?"

She turned to her computer monitor and started typing, as if she might be able to conjure up Mark by running some commands. "What room are you staying in?"

"Five nineteen." Pearce inspected the lobby again. Mark would come walking in the door any minute, sunburned and tired from having walked so far along the beach. Pearce just knew it.

"I show you are here with us for another four nights," the clerk said.

"Yes, through Sunday." Pearce discovered he was tapping the room key card on the counter, and stuffed it into his pocket. "It's just, I haven't seen him—my friend—since breakfast this morning, and he didn't leave a note or anything, so I'm a little worried."

"I see. What does your friend look like?"

"He's a little shorter than me, about five feet ten, with blond hair and blue eyes. His name's Mark Beecher."

"American too, yes?"

"Yes. That's right. American." Pearce nodded as hope simmered to life within his chest. She had seen Mark. "Did you see him down here in the lobby at some point recently?"

The clerk shook her head. "No, I'm sorry, sir. I just came on duty only a short while ago. I don't recall seeing someone fitting that description. Do you want me to contact hotel security for you?"

Pearce let out a breath. "No, not yet. I'll go around the hotel and look for him. Maybe we just missed each other at the room."

"Of course, sir. I'm sorry you can't locate your friend." The clerk appeared appropriately saddened by Pearce's predicament. "I'm sure he's off seeing sights and just lost track of the time."

"Yeah. That's probably it."

Pearce turned to go, and the woman said, "Please let us know if we can be of further assistance."

Pearce nodded. "I will. Thanks." He walked through the lobby to check the souvenir shop and then stepped out to the pool before making another pass along the beach. Still no sign of Mark, and now a small kernel of dread had begun to form within his concern.

CHAPTER 9

The hotel security man, Isaiah, was taller than Pearce, at least six feet six, and he covered a lot of ground with each step. As they walked around the hotel, Pearce found himself hurrying to keep up, something he was not used to.

"How long has it been since you've seen him?" Isaiah asked.

"Um, since midmorning," Pearce replied. "We were at breakfast."

"You're good friends?" Isaiah glanced at Pearce from the corner of his eye.

Pearce simply replied, "Yes," reluctant to reveal the true nature of their relationship in a foreign country where homosexuality was punishable by life in prison.

"Lovers?" Isaiah pushed.

Pearce came to a stop and stared at the security guard. "What?"

"My line of questioning makes you uncomfortable," Isaiah stated.

"I don't want you to get distracted from the fact that a man is missing," Pearce explained. "I would hope the nature of our rela-tionship would not be a factor in how much effort you put into finding him. And just so you know, back in the States, I am a special agent for the FBI."

Isaiah raised his eyebrows, and Pearce continued. "I just want to find my friend, okay? Yes, Mark and I are lovers. No, I do not know where he is at this time, and I have not heard from him for pretty much the entire day, and it's after six now. This is very unlike him, and I am concerned something's happened to him. Is there any way to check the hospitals or police stations? See if he might be hurt or something?"

A solemn nod from Isaiah made Pearce relax, at least a little, and they continued to walk. There was no sign of Mark at the pool, on the beach, or in the bar. They checked the room again, where Pearce showed Isaiah that Mark's clothes were all in place as well as his shaving kit.

"All that you are showing me does seem to point to Mr. Beecher not leaving the island on his own." Isaiah opened his hands, his light pink palms a stark contrast to the dark pigment of the tops. "I can lodge a report with the Royal Barbados Police Force and inquire at the local hospitals if you like."

"Yes, please. And let me know what information you need from me."

"Of course, Mr. Pearce. And please let me know should you hear anything about Mr. Beecher's whereabouts or condition."

Pearce pressed his lips tight together. "I will. And please do the same for me."

"Absolutely I will, Mr. Pearce. I will be in touch soon. Thank you."

After the door had closed behind Isaiah, Pearce sat on the edge of the mattress and put his head in his hands. He thought about the argument he and Mark had had in the dining room, and wondered if Mark had seen it as serious enough to leave him, just walk out and find somewhere to go without taking any of his things with him.

But that was ridiculous. Mark was a planner; he even planned out the routes for his errands, starting at the farthest spot and working his way back home.

A thought occurred to Pearce, and he pushed up from the mattress to cross the room to the closet doors, then pulled them open. The room safe sat on the floor of the closet, and Pearce punched in the combination they had chosen: 0116, the day they had first met at the FBI building in Detroit. The door popped open, and Pearce reached inside. Both of their cell phones, Mark's iPod, and both their wallets lay within the safe. He picked up and held Mark's wallet tightly, brought it to his forehead, and closed his eyes, as if by clutching the collection of plastic cards, ID, and cash that so defined Mark and wishing hard enough, he could make him appear. After a moment, Pearce lowered his hand and looked at the wallet.

"So you didn't leave me," he whispered. "I'll find you. Just hold on, Mark, and I'll find you."

ISAIAH CALLED the room an hour later with the news that no man matching Mark's description had been checked in to the hospitals. The police had no information either, and Isaiah wanted to search around the hotel grounds once again. Pearce met the man in the lobby, and together they walked out to the pool deck. It was seven in the evening, and people were drifting back outside to watch the sunset or heading to dinner. Pearce recalled the dinner he and Mark had shared the night before, wished he'd taken more time to simply enjoy being with Mark and savor their time together. He really needed to get better at recognizing the important, quiet moments and pay attention to them, hoard them away inside to keep with him.

There was a line at the scooter rental booth, and Pearce had a sudden thought that Mark might have checked out another bike. He said as much to Isaiah, and they approached the scooter booth to wait as the kid running it checked in a young couple. When the couple walked off hand in hand, the kid looked at Pearce and said, "Hey, five nineteen! You want a scooter now too?"

Pearce felt as if a bucket of ice water had been dumped over his head. "Did you rent a scooter to my friend today?"

The kid looked from Pearce to Isaiah and back again before giving a solemn nod.

"You're certain it was Mr. Beecher who rented a scooter this morning?" Isaiah asked.

"Yeah, room five nineteen," the kid said and turned away to check a computer screen. "Checked it out at ten forty-eight this morning. He's overdue now." He said to Pearce, "I'll have to charge you for another day. Sorry."

Pearce shook his head, his thoughts spinning and colliding and fragmenting. Mark had stormed out of the dining room without his wallet and rented a scooter. He suspected Mark had gone back to the Bridgetown Bar, and why he hadn't thought about it before, Pearce had no idea. He supposed he had been too focused on finding Mark somewhere in the vicinity of the hotel.

"He went back there," Pearce said and closed his eyes as he tightened his hands into fists.

"Mr. Pearce?" Isaiah asked. "Do you know where Mr. Beecher is now?"

Pearce met the security guard's gaze. "I might have an idea. I think he might have gone into Bridgetown to a local bar we stopped at a few days ago."

"With no wallet?" Isaiah asked. "What makes you so sure of this?"

"When we were there before, we saw a trio of young girls. One of them was a blonde American girl who reminded Mark of someone he had known back home. Something seemed off about their situation, and he was concerned the girls might be held against their will."

"Which bar?" the scooter rental kid asked.

"The Bridgetown Bar," Pearce replied.

The kid nodded and shrugged. "Tough place. Yeah, could be."

Isaiah said to the kid in a clipped voice, "Thank you for your help. You may close up now." Then he turned to Pearce and gestured for him to walk with him back toward the hotel door. When they were out of earshot of the scooter rental booth, Isaiah said, "You suspected the girls were being forced into sex?"

"Mark wondered about it," Pearce replied. "He had known a girl in high school who disappeared on a senior trip to an island. They never found a trace of her or a body."

"Natalee Holloway?" Isaiah asked, and Pearce felt a cold twinge of nerves. Everyone knew the name of one girl who had vanished, but what about all the others who went missing? What became of them as well?

"No, before her. She had a unique name. I can't recall it now." Pearce looked out at the water, where the lowering sun seemed to set fire to the ocean. "The girl reminded him of her, and he became a little obsessed with her. Thought she might be in trouble."

"Did you contact the Royal Barbados Police Force?"

"No." Pearce shook his head and had to force down a hot, acidic sense of guilt. "I told him we had no power here on the island. I said we were just visitors and weren't sure of the girl's background and history." Pearce let out a frustrated breath. "Damn it, I didn't think he'd go back there alone."

"You were there what day?" Isaiah asked.

"Yesterday. Well, the day before was when we saw the girl out on the porch, and then yesterday we went inside and asked questions."

"You questioned these people on your own?" Isaiah's eyebrows shot up.

"I know, I know," Pearce said with a tired nod. "We should have gone to the police. But I've questioned people before—a lot of people. It's part of my job as an agent."

"Of course, sir, but as you stated before, you are out of your jurisdiction here in Barbados," Isaiah said. "I need to contact the RBPF again, give them this new information. He may have had an accident on the scooter, or something may have happened at the bar. Come inside to my office, and we'll place the call."

"Can we go to the Bridgetown Bar first?" Pearce asked. "Talking to the police will take some time, and I don't know that we've got a lot of it left."

"Sadly the Bridgetown Bar is off hotel grounds and out of my influence of power," Isaiah said. "But come, let's contact the RBPF and have you speak to a detective there."

"How about you contact the police for me," Pearce suggested. "You can tell them what's going on and let them know I'm going to the Bridgetown Bar, and they can meet me there."

Isaiah furrowed his brow. "That would not be the standard way we conduct an investigation."

Pearce backed two steps away from the security guard, glad he had grabbed his wallet from the safe before leaving the room. "Sometimes, Isaiah, you have to step outside the bounds of what's considered standard. Believe me, if I've learned anything as an agent, it's that one thing." He turned his back on the security guard and jogged down the path to the circular drive of the front of the hotel, heading for the cabstand.

THE RIDE to the Bridgetown Bar seemed to take an eternity. Pearce sat in the backseat, bouncing his leg and tapping his fingers on his knee. The skin on the back of his thigh, damp with nervous sweat, stuck to the vinyl seat and made a slick ripping sound with each bounce.

"American?" the cabdriver asked, his dark eyes darting up to the mirror to peer at Pearce.

What the hell was it with everyone asking where he was from? Was this how foreigners were treated back in the States?

"Yeah, American," Pearce said.

"What city?"

"Washington, DC."

The cabdriver's eyes lit up. "The nation's capital!"

Pearce couldn't help grinning. "Yes, exactly. The nation's capital."

"You know Obama?"

That brought up a laugh. "No, I don't know Obama."

The cabdriver seemed truly disappointed. "Too bad. Obama is a rock star."

"That he is," Pearce muttered. "That he is. We almost there?"

"Almost. Not far. How about Hillary Clinton? You know her?"

After several more questions, Pearce was grateful when the cab pulled into the shared parking lot of the Flying Fish Eatery and the Bridgetown Bar, the white gravel crunching under the car's tires. He tossed the man double what was on the meter and followed it with, "Please wait," as he got out.

"You got it, American buddy!" the cabdriver called back.

Pearce walked fast, stones grinding grittily beneath his shoes as he crossed the parking lot to the porch. He heard music from the jukebox and people laughing and talking over the sound of it as he reached for the door handle. When Pearce stepped inside, a dozen pairs of eyes turned at once to take him in, and all conversation died.

He was the minority, and he understood how African Americans must feel back home as he made his way between the tables toward the bar. The big bartender Pearce had talked with the day before—Abraham?—glared at him as he approached, and two couples moved aside to allow Pearce to step up close to the bar.

"Have you seen my friend?" Pearce raised his voice to be heard over the music.

Abraham continued to glare at him. "Who are you talking about?"

"My friend I was in here with yesterday. The blond man, just a little shorter than me, wearing glasses. We were just in here yesterday asking you questions about the girl on the porch. His name is Mark Beecher, and I know he came here on his own today."

"Haven't seen any blond man today," Abraham said. "You're the only white man who's set foot in here all day."

Pearce leaned in over the bar and felt the man to either side of him step closer. "Look. I know he came back here. He was worried about the girl we saw yesterday. He came back here to find out about her, see if she was all right. Just tell me where he is, and I'll take him away, and we'll be done, okay? No RBPF, no other trouble. I just want to take him back to the hotel."

Abraham twisted up the corner of his lip with disgust. "Bulla men need to be careful here in Barbados. You should go."

"Where's Mark?" Pearce demanded.

"I haven't seen him. Don't know anything about any blonde girl either, and sure as hell don't know nothing about some bulla American."

Pearce reacted without thinking. He reached across the bar and grabbed Abraham's shirt, yanking the bastard up against the bar and close to his face. The song on the jukebox ended, allowing Pearce to hear the shouts of alarm behind him and the scrape of chair legs as the patrons got to their feet. Strong hands grabbed him by the arms, but he clung to Abraham's shirt long enough to say in a low growl, "Give him back to me, goddamn it, or you'll all fucking regret it."

Before the bartender could respond, Pearce was pulled away by a group of men. Their hands were calloused and damp with sweat as they shoved him toward the door. Someone punched the back of his head, sending black dots swarming across his vision, and someone else drove a fist into his gut. The air left his lungs in a painful whoosh and doubled him over, and the group dragged him the rest of the way across the floor. They pushed out the screen door and dumped him on the porch, leaving him gasping for breath on the smooth, faded boards. A kick to his left side, right over his kidney, sent a shock of pain up his back, and he cried out.

"My friend! Oh no, my friend!" It was the cabdriver, kneeling beside him, hands fluttering over him as if trying to decide where to light first. "What happened? You all right?"

A siren wailed in the distance. Perfect.

"RBPF is on its way," the cabdriver said. "Stay or go, friend? It's up to you."

With some effort, Pearce pushed himself into a seated position. His stomach rolled threateningly, and a dull pain radiated down the back of his neck, not to mention the bass-drum throb in his right shoulder from his old injury. He was way too young to feel like this after a simple bar beating.

Pearce glared up into the cabdriver's face and said around his clenched jaw, "We're staying. I'm finding Mark and taking him back with me."

CHAPTER 10

His arm hurt. That was all Mark could seem to focus on as he lay stretched out in the back of the van. He'd been in the vehicle all day, coming to now and then, his lips and throat dry as the sun burned down on the top of the van, cooking him. The engine was choppy—something was off with the timing—and the sound and vibration of travel lulled him back under each time he awoke.

Now, however, he could see it was dark outside the van's windows. A tiny alarm rang in a distant corner of his mind, barely registering as his thoughts came together, shattered apart, drifted around, and came back together again. Where was Aaron? Was he here with him? Had they rented a van to drive around the island?

A spark of memory returned. The motor scooter ride into Bridgetown. He'd been alone, and he'd had a specific destination in mind. But where? And why had he been alone?

The spark lit a fuse that sizzled through the darkness in his mind, lighting up more memories. The bar. The girl on the porch at the bar. She'd been hurt, and he'd tried to step in.

"We're taking him to the house, yeah?"

The voice was deep and startled him. Mark didn't recognize the speaker, and he felt the first real tremor of fear since coming around. What was happening to him?

"Yeah, the house. Said he knows a buyer who'll pay big money for an American man."

"Think it's different?"

"What?"

"Fucking an asshole rather than a pussy."

"You going to try it?"

The men laughed, the sound of it sending shivers through Mark. There was no humor in those laughs, just cruelty.

"Yeah, I'd try it. Might try that nice piece back there once we get him to the house."

"Better not ruin him before the sale. Abraham will tear up *your* bulla hole."

More laughter, and Mark was starting to truly understand the depth of danger he had fallen into. He'd been taken by sex slavers, and they were talking about auctioning him off to the highest bidder.

Mark shifted position and gasped. His left arm ached, the pain radiating up from his elbow. Something was wrong, something in his skin, right in the crook of his elbow. Every time he tried to move his arm, he felt a sharp pain. He lifted his arm and forced his eyes open, then realized he'd lost his glasses. He'd have to find them later; for now he needed to see what was wrong with his arm, because he had to get out of this van and away from these men.

A tube ran into his arm and ended in a wide piece of tape at the inside of his elbow. He squinted and tipped his head back, following the tube to its source: an IV bag. The sight brought everything clear in a jolt of terror. He was being drugged and taken somewhere to be auctioned off, and after that he would be raped.

He had to escape.

"He's up again." One of the voices from the front of the van spoke once more.

"Shit. Give him another, then," the second voice said.

"Third time today," the hard voice said. "Think it'll kill him?"

"Nah, he'll be fine. Just dose him. I don't want him talking anymore. That was fucking creepy."

"All right."

Mark heard someone move around, then felt the tube attached to his arm swing as someone took hold of it, the cool length brushing against his left arm. He flinched and drew in a hiss of breath between his teeth at the spark of pain his sudden movement caused, but then a moment later, the pain faded away, and he drifted into darkness.

PEARCE STOOD with his hands on his hips and his head down, staring at the gravel beneath his sneakers. The stones glowed white in the shine of the police car's headlights. "No. I did not accost anyone."

"Abraham here says you reached across the bar and grabbed his shirt." The officer of the Royal Barbados Police Force gestured to the big, slump-shouldered form of the bartender. "Did you do that?"

Pearce raised his gaze and tried to keep his voice calm and even. "Look, I already told you, I'm searching for my friend, Mark Beecher. I'm certain he checked a motor scooter out from our hotel and rode it to this bar to see about a girl we saw here a couple of days ago. Okay? Isaiah, the head of security at our hotel, already called this in and made a report."

"I don't know about any report," the officer said. "When was this call?"

"I'm not sure." Pearce tried hard to not get frustrated. "I wasn't with him when he called. It was sometime this afternoon, maybe early evening. Something like that."

"Your friend told you this was where he was headed?" the officer asked.

"No. He just walked off, but I know he would have come here." Pearce put his hands on top of his head and flinched at the pull in his right shoulder, a souvenir of his trip to Detroit when he had first met Mark. Memories of that time flashed through his mind—being with Mark in the loft, getting to know him, making love with him, and then Robert Morgan taking Pearce to that abandoned house and stabbing him. He let out his breath, forced those memories aside, and focused on the RBPF officer once again. "Can you please just look around the bar? Maybe check up and down the block for the motor scooter? It has to be here somewhere."

"What type of scooter?"

"A Vespa," Pearce said. "Yellow. It was the same one he rode yesterday, according to the kid at the rental booth."

The officer turned to speak to another officer, younger, and Pearce watched the man hurry back to the police car. The younger officer grabbed a flashlight from the glove box, switched it on, and jogged to the back of the bar, the beam swaying and bouncing in front of him.

"Good. Thank you." Pearce nodded with relief.

"Now, about your treatment of Abraham here," the officer said. "You grabbed hold of him first. Do you agree?"

Pearce waved at the officer, his attention focused on the rear of the bar, where he could see the flashlight beam shining over shrubs and the Dumpster at the back of the property. "Yeah, I grabbed him." He turned to the man and slouched a bit, trying to appear like less of a threat. "I know how this looks, but Abraham knows something about where my friend is, okay? He does. Something is going on in this bar that you need to know about."

"This is our job, sir," the officer said, his voice cool and clipped. "That's why we are here. We are investigating your claims. But you have to realize that Abraham has claims of his own."

Before Pearce could respond, the young officer jogged back toward them, the flashlight bobbing in front of him. He came to a stop and said to the older officer, "No scooter back there, sir."

"I told you," Abraham said, throwing his meaty arms over his head. "He just wants to cause me trouble."

Pearce rolled his eyes and turned in a circle. He knew men like Abraham—knew them well. He had chased down smarter men than Abraham back home. But back home, he also had a partner and the resources of the FBI to lean on. Here he was on his own, and he didn't even have Mark to talk with about it all.

Besides that, Pearce couldn't be sure the officers before him weren't being paid by Abraham to look the other way. Corruption could permeate all throughout the Royal Barbados Police Force. How was he to know?

"There is no scooter behind the bar, Mr. Pearce," the older officer said, as if Pearce hadn't been standing right there listening when the younger man had reported back.

"Yeah, I got that." Pearce took a deep breath and tipped back his head to look up at the stars. Had it only been three nights ago that he and Mark were having sex on the beach beneath these same stars? He exhaled and then said to the officer, "I'd like to open a missing persons case."

The officer pressed his lips together but then gave a nod. "You're lucky Abraham's not pressing assault charges against you, but come to the station with me, and a detective will write up the report."

"Good. Thank you." Pearce stalked past Abraham without another word and slid into the backseat of the small police car. The cabdriver had left an hour ago, glad to get away from any entanglement with the RBPF, and Pearce envied him. He knew taking the time to file a missing persons report was necessary, but Pearce couldn't help feeling like he was wasting precious time he could be spending trying to track Mark down.

But where would he start? He was just one man on a foreign island, and he had never felt so alone in his entire life.

CHAPTER 11

After filing a missing persons report with a detective named Dominik Arnott, Pearce was given a ride back to the hotel. He walked the beach and prowled through the hotel bar, looking for Mark or someone acting suspicious. All he saw, however, were drunk, happy, relaxed vacationers and the tired but alert servers who waited on them.

It was late when Pearce finally returned to the room. There was no sign that Mark had been back, and Pearce changed into black jeans and a black T-shirt. If he was going to snoop around at night, he didn't want any ID on him. He took some of the cash out of his wallet and then put the wallet in the safe with Mark's.

He stood by the window a moment, wishing he had his gun with him. He knew that anything could have happened to Mark—an accident along the road, robbery, or that he ran the scooter out of gas—but Pearce was more than certain Mark had gone back to the bar, and that was where he would start. With that decided, he left the room and headed for the cabstand.

He had the cabdriver drop him off down the block from the bar and walked back. It was late now, at least midnight, so the Flying

Fish Eatery was closed, but the Bridgetown Bar was in full swing. Music and laughter and conversation poured through the screen door, and on the porch, two couples stood close together, making out.

Pearce made his way around the far side of the Flying Fish Eatery to the alley in the back and then moved as quietly as possible over the gravel to the back of the Bridgetown Bar. The door to the kitchen of the bar stood open to let in the cool night air, and the smell of hot grease and fried fish made his stomach rumble. He hadn't eaten dinner, and his hunger was starting to catch up with him.

An apron of light spilled through the screen door leading into the kitchen, and Pearce moved slowly around the illuminated area, keeping his head down and scanning back and forth. He'd done this so many times for cases back home, walking the grid of a crime scene, looking for any possible evidence—bullet casings, footprints, cigarette butts. He didn't know what, if anything, he expected to find, but he had to start somewhere.

The light from the doorway faded into darkness as it stretched toward a rusted Dumpster. As Pearce approached it, the stench of rotting food hit him like a slap in the face, and he winced. He knew he should check inside the Dumpster but hesitated. There was just enough shadow across the top of it to make him think the interior would be even darker. And he had forgotten to bring a flashlight.

Still, he had to at least lift the lid to find out what he could see inside. If Mark was in there—hurt or, well, worse—he wouldn't forgive himself for not looking. So he approached the front of the Dumpster and extended a hand toward the heavy plastic lid as he breathed through his mouth. Just before he reached it, Pearce stepped on something that shifted beneath his shoe, and he stopped. It was too dark for him to see what it was, so he crouched down to pick it up.

A low gasp slipped out as he held up a flip-flop. It was coated in dust, and when Pearce turned it over to look at the bottom, he couldn't keep in the quiet cry of anguish when he saw the plastic bread-bag tag holding the toe separator in place.

This was Mark's flip-flop! Mark had been here, and now Pearce knew for certain this was where he'd run into trouble.

A sound from behind brought him around as his heart pounded. All he saw was a hulking silhouette and then felt a blow against the side of his head. Pearce fell to the gravel, disoriented, the pain a jagged spike of heat inside his skull. He knew he had to get up and fight back, knew he couldn't stay on the ground, but when he tried to push up to all fours, a wave of dizziness made the ground spin beneath him.

Footsteps came up behind him, and with great effort, Pearce kicked out, grimly satisfied when he felt his foot connect with his attacker's shin. He heard a grunt of pain and then, in the light from the Bridgetown Bar's open back door, saw another man's foot pull back for a kick. Before he could react, he felt the kick connect and fell down into blackness.

PEARCE STARTED awake and looked around. He was in a hospital bed, an IV in his arm and the fast beeping of a heart monitor just behind his head. When he sat up, a ragged pain sparked to life inside his head, and nausea knotted his stomach. He fell back onto the mattress and closed his eyes, focusing his thoughts on not vomiting. Pearce really hated to get sick.

The door opened, and a nurse walked in, smiling at the sight of him awake.

"Well, hello there," she said in a cheerful voice. "Look who's back among the living."

"Where…?" Pearce tried to ask but couldn't get the words out.

But the nurse knew what he wanted to know and, as she checked his IV drip, said, "You're in Queen Elizabeth Hospital."

"Mark?" Pearce managed to rasp.

The nurse frowned at him. "Is that your name? You had no ID on you, so we've got you listed as John Doe."

Pearce shook his head. "Aaron Pearce."

"That you?"

He nodded, his throat too dry to talk much, so he asked, "Water?"

She poured water from a pitcher into a cup, dropped in a straw, and handed it to him. The water was cold and washed over his raw throat in soothing waves. As he drank, the nurse continued to explain.

"You were dropped off in emergency, blood all over your face and no money or ID on you. The doctor cleaned you up and took X-rays."

When Pearce tried to recall what had happened, all he could remember was being in the hotel room. He'd been planning to go out—he knew that much—but where? And for what?

"Who?" Pearce handed her the empty glass for a refill. "Who dropped me off?"

"A nice man," she said as she refilled his cup. "He owns the Flying Fish Eatery. Said he heard a fight from behind the bar next door as he was locking up his restaurant and called out. When he got to you, whoever did this was gone. He brought you here himself."

Pearce nodded; the name of the restaurant sounded familiar. Then a sliver of a memory lit up inside his aching head: he'd been there with Mark. Another spark ignited, and he remembered that Mark was missing. He'd gone there looking for Mark. He felt a chill and heard the heart monitor speed up as he turned to the nurse and asked, "How long have I been here?"

"All last night and half of today," she said, eyeing the monitor. "Lie back, honey, and relax. You've got a concussion and a nasty bruise on your temple."

"My... Mark, my friend, is missing. I need to find him."

"You can't go anywhere," she said. "Not with a concussion."

Pearce slid his legs out from under the sheet and tried to sit up. His sense of balance deserted him, leaving him dizzy and nauseated again, more so than before. The nurse managed to hand him a plastic tray just in time for Pearce to lean forward and throw up.

Damn it, he hated throwing up.

Pain thundered through his head with each clench of his stomach, and suddenly all the strength went out of him. He sagged to the side and remained awake long enough to feel the nurse grab him by the shoulders before he went under again.

WHEN PEARCE AWOKE AGAIN, a man who looked familiar stood at the foot of his bed with the nurse. Pearce's throat burned, and a dull pain throbbed across the top of his skull. He cleared his throat and tried to sit up, but the man and the nurse moved to either side of him to gently push him back against the mattress. Pearce rolled his head on the pillow to stare up at the man, and recognition clicked just before the man spoke.

"Hello, Mr. Pearce. Do you know who I am?"

Pearce nodded, then flinched at the line of pain that crackled down the base of his skull and into his neck. "Yeah. Detective Arnott, RBPF."

"Yes, correct. Do you know who you are?"

Pearce glared at him. "Aaron Pearce, FBI."

"Very good. Now, do you know who did this to you?" Arnott asked.

"No. It was dark. I couldn't see them."

"Do you remember where you were?"

Pearce thought a moment. Where had he been? Near a bar, but why? Then it all came back, and he tried to sit up again, but once more the nurse and Arnott pushed him back down. "Mark. Did you find Mark? How long have I been here? Was Mark there?"

"Easy now, Mr. Pearce," Arnott said. "One thing at a time. You have been here since last night. It is now early evening. And no, we have not yet found Mr. Beecher. You were attacked behind the Bridgetown Bar near a Dumpster. Do you remember why you were there?"

Pearce closed his eyes. "I was looking for Mark. For a clue about what happened."

"I see. Even though RBPF officers have already investigated the bar?"

Pearce opened his eyes to meet Arnott's gaze. "I found Mark's flip-flop by the Dumpster before I was attacked."

Arnott's eyebrows went up. "You are certain it belonged to Mr. Beecher?"

Pearce recalled Mark showing him how he had fixed the flip-flops he had just bought to make them last a little longer. And what Pearce wouldn't give right now to have Mark back in the hotel with him, leaving those same fucking shoes in the middle of the room to trip him up. Pearce took a breath and said, "I'm sure it was Mark's. He'd just bought them in the hotel gift shop, and the toe divider came apart, so he fixed it with a bread tag."

"I see." Arnott nodded to the nurse, and she turned away to leave the room.

"You know something," Pearce said.

"No, Mr. Pearce, I know nothing more than I did before I found you here." The detective shrugged. "You were attacked behind the Bridgetown Bar after midnight. I have questioned the bar owner, Abraham, and he knows nothing of the crime and has witnesses who state he was inside the bar at the time of the attack."

Pearce clenched his jaw, felt the ache in his head intensify, and forced himself to stop. "Of course he does. So there are no witnesses to what happened to me?"

"Unfortunately no," Arnott replied. "The owner of the Flying Fish Eatery interrupted the fight but did not see your attackers. We have checked the area behind the Bridgetown Bar very thoroughly but did not find a flip-flop as you have described."

"Well, that's not a surprise," Pearce grumbled. He pushed himself up in the bed, closing his eyes as pain swept through his skull. When it abated, he asked, "When can I get out of here?"

"That, Mr. Pearce, is up to the doctor." Arnott turned for the door. "You are fortunate that your injuries are not more serious. It was only by luck that I happened to see the incident report on the investigating officer's desk and through that found you here. If it were up to me, I would keep you here for at least one more day to allow me to continue my investigation without worrying about you getting yourself into more trouble."

"I'm not staying here another night," Pearce said to Arnott's back as the detective walked into the hall. When the door had shut, Pearce pushed aside the covers and slid his feet over the edge of the mattress. The linoleum was cold under his bare feet, and the touch of it made him shiver. He closed his eyes as gooseflesh rippled across his body and he was swamped with dizziness. The room seemed to tilt, and he stayed upright only by gripping the sheet beneath him tight with his fists.

"You're not going anywhere."

Pearce opened his eyes and found the nurse standing before him, a stern expression on her face. "You can't even stand up on your own. You'll do your missing friend no good if you leave here too soon. Get back into bed. Don't make me go get Donald to come strap you in."

"I need to be out there," Pearce said, but his voice came out in a dry whisper as his stomach rolled.

"You need to rest. Come on, now. Doctor will see you soon."

Pearce tried to push up off the bed to prove the nurse wrong but felt something tug on his arm, followed by a quick spike of pain. He realized as the floor went out from under him that he'd forgotten to pull out his IV needle, and he blacked out before he could curse.

CHAPTER 12

"If you move too fast or too slow, I will stick this knife in your spine, and you'll never walk again."

The voice was low, steady, and terrifying. Mark swallowed hard and stepped forward. The cement was rough beneath his feet, and the cool air of the dark hallway washed over him, leaving his skin covered in goose bumps. He was nude, and his brain wasn't moving at its normal pace. The walls to either side of him seemed to be less than solid, and the shadows around him looked thick and substantial. Since he'd lost his glasses somewhere along the way, everything and everyone had slightly feathered edges, but Mark also knew he had been drugged. The dull ache in his left arm was a key indicator of that, as well as the taste of medicine-laced cotton along his tongue.

"Where?" he managed to ask, feeling like the single word tore up his throat as he forced it out.

"Don't you worry about that," the man behind him said. "You just walk until I tell you to stop."

Mark tried to think about what had happened. He knew the details would be important later, would be needed for him to be considered a credible witness. He could remember coming upon the girl with a group of men behind the Bridgetown Bar. One man had pulled a gun and had talked with the others about killing him. The girl had grabbed him—he clearly remembered that—and then something had been said about selling him before he had been roughed up, and then…? Nothing. Only impressions of moments, really, like wisps of dreams that floated just out of reach after he'd awakened. He had to have been drugged this entire time, but he wasn't even sure how long he'd been gone or where he was. For all he knew, they could have taken him off Barbados by now.

But a stubborn blaze of hope burned to life, starting from a small place deep inside his chest. Pearce. If anyone would be able to find him, Pearce could do it. Even though they'd argued—even though Mark now knew he'd been so wrong about how to approach his suspicions—he was sure Pearce would find him. With all the years of training and investigative experience he possessed, with all his stubborn bullheadedness, Pearce would not stop looking until he found Mark.

"Stop." The man behind tapped hard on the back of his head, and Mark flinched as he came to a stop. A dozen feet ahead of him, the hall ended at a dirt-streaked window. To his right was a closed door, the red paint that had once covered it flaked and peeling away from its dark, softening wood beneath. Mark stared at the window, then turned to the door. The paint wasn't just flaking off the wood, it was marred with long, jagged cracks.

The door was yanked open, startling him, and he saw two men flanking the doorway to a small room. The man behind Mark gave his bare ass a stinging slap, making him jump, and Mark hurried into the room.

Lights flared to life, blinding and buzzing, and Mark squinted against the sudden glare. Four men stood around the small room, all of them watching him with menacing grins. A couple of them let out hard laughter that frightened him as much as any threat of violence had so far. On one side of him, a young girl, also nude, with light auburn hair and glazed blue eyes, was being led by the arm toward the door through which he had just entered.

Mark noted that at the corner farthest from the door, a low, raised platform had been built in front of a heavy red velvet wall hanging. Lights were set up on tripods around the platform, and centered in front of it was a camera on a tripod with wires running out the back of it.

"Move," the man behind him said, his voice gruff and the finger he poked into Mark's ribs tipped with a sharp nail.

As he walked toward the platform, Mark felt the heat of the lights, heard the buzz of them within his head as if a tiny hive of bees lived inside his ears. He stopped at the edge of the platform and had to concentrate a moment to get his right foot to lift high enough from the floor for him to step up. He lost his balance, however, and he would have fallen over if not for the man behind him. Rough, strong hands grabbed him under the arms, shoved him up onto the platform, and then spun him to face the camera.

"Item eight-five-four, a new arrival," said a man from somewhere beyond the lights. "And not our usual fare. He is sure to please those who possess a more varied palate. American, as you can see, in good shape and apparently a true blond."

Laughter roared around the room as Mark stood blinking under the bright lights. A tiny red light glowed on the camera, and he stared at it, letting it ground him. He knew he needed to get out of this place, away from these men, but he wasn't able to put enough thoughts together to form some kind of escape plan, a way to get back to Pearce. Or at least get a message to Pearce to tell him where to come save him.

A low ringing sound brought Mark out of his contemplation, and he watched as, at the back of the room, the outline of a man lifted his hand to speak into a phone. Was this really happening, or was this some strange dream from which he was unable to awaken? He felt disconnected, as though he stood two feet behind his body, watching himself move.

"Your client number, please," said the man at the back of the room.

Mark closed his eyes and tried to corral his thoughts. He needed to let anyone watching know that he was in trouble, that he needed help. It took a great deal of concentration, but he finally managed to form the words in his brain, and then he said, "Help me," in a dry, croaking voice.

"And your bid, please?" asked the man on the phone.

They were taking bids on him, auctioning him off like an animal, like livestock. He was nothing more than a piece of meat to them, something to corral and transport and deliver. And whomever they delivered him to would treat him even worse. These men wanted their money's worth, so they weren't going to harm him in any way that would leave a mark. But that was no guarantee from the highest bidder.

If he was going to escape, he would need to do it here, before he was turned over to whoever won this sinister auction.

"Thank you," said the man at the back of the room. "I have your bid noted."

"Turn around," someone to his right whispered.

"What?" Mark asked, his voice a quiet rasp as he searched the room for the speaker. "What did you say?"

"Turn around," the voice repeated. "In a circle."

Mark looked down at his feet, considered them a moment, and then willed them to move. He turned in a circle, watching his feet the whole time.

"Jesus Christ, do it slower!" the man snapped. "It's not a fucking line dance."

Mark kept his gaze on his feet. He took a breath and made himself turn in a circle once more, slower this time. As he turned, tears welled up, and he forced them back. He would not cry; these men would get off on that way too much. He thought of the dozens, maybe hundreds, of girls who had been sold by these men, and the anger that ignited within him helped push back the fear. He needed to stay strong, stay alert, and keep his eye open for any chance of escape.

As he finished the turn, Mark took the opportunity to check out the room. There were two windows, both covered with cardboard, and just the one door to leave and enter. If he was going to try to get away, Mark knew the best time would be out in the hallway, when just one man would be with him. He needed to focus his attention, keep his thoughts sharp, and let them believe he was out of it. For him to have a chance, he needed them to not see him as a possible escapee.

"Good. See? He can be trained," the man said, and the others around him laughed.

When he faced the camera once again, Mark stared into the lens, gathered his strength, and said as loud and clear as he could, "My name is Mark Beecher, and I'm being held against my will."

Something struck him on the back of the head, and Mark dropped to his knees on the dark, scarred wood of the platform. A sunburst of pain flared inside his skull, and tears filled his eyes as he lifted a hand to touch the sore spot.

He heard two men yelling back and forth, one of them shouting about the condition of the merchandise and the other about training the merchandise. As the argument continued, Mark used the time to slowly roll his eyes up to look around the room while keeping his head bowed. The edges of everything around him were blurred without his glasses, but he saw four men—all Bajan—the video camera, its red light now off, and a few chairs scattered about.

No one stood near the door.

Oddly, the blow to his head had awakened him somehow, sharpened his senses. Now he just needed an opportunity. With slow movements, Mark rose to his feet and swayed unsteadily. He reached out a hand and stumbled toward a chair close to the door.

"You there, stop!" a man shouted.

"He's going to sit down, is all," another explained.

Mark sat in the chair, going down more heavily than needed to appear like less of a threat. Once he got into the hallway outside the room, he'd need to find the door leading outside and escape. The shouts around him had now escalated into a full-out argument, and Mark turned sideways on the chair to angle his body toward the door. He wasn't sure how he would open the door and slip out without someone noticing, but all he would need was seconds to get out of the room.

His ears rang from the blow to the back of his head, and when he reached back once again to touch the tender spot, he drew in a hissing breath at the pain. There was no blood, so the skin wasn't broken, but he'd have a goose egg for sure. This, he knew, was the least of his worries, but he milked the reaction to make himself seem more injured than he truly was in case anyone was watching him.

The door opened, and a girl stumbled inside. She was nude, her head down, chin to her chest, a long mane of brunette hair hanging over her face. A man behind her pushed her farther into the room, and she fell to the floor on her hands and knees, the tan lines just above the pale cheeks of her ass testament to the vacation she had been enjoying before she'd been taken. Most of the men in the room snickered and called out such comments as "four on the floor" and "doggy style," but two of the men shouted for them to be careful with the merchandise.

Red-hot fury erupted inside Mark, and he clenched his jaw as his leg muscles tightened. He tore his gaze from the girl and noticed the door stood ajar, just enough for him to fit through. Mark saw the men were focused entirely on the girl, and he knew this would be his only chance. He pushed up off the chair. Keeping his gaze locked on the door, he took a step toward it. His heart pounded and the nerves throughout his body tingled like a latticework of fear. No one said anything, so he took another step. And then another. His pulse beat in his ears, and the spot on his head where he'd been struck throbbed in time.

He reached the door and extended his hand. He did not look behind him. He didn't want to see one of the men reaching for him, his mouth an ugly snarl of anger. There was no shout for him to stop, and Mark stepped up to the narrow opening in the doorway and slipped through.

It had been easier than he had thought to get out the door unseen. The men inside were still arguing over or mocking the new arrival. Mark didn't hesitate once he stepped into the hallway. He looked right and left, squinting to try and make sense of the heavily shadowed hall. He'd come from the left and knew there was a stairway around the corner; he'd seen that much when he'd been brought to the room. But he was afraid more men would be waiting at the foot of those stairs, guarding the "merchandise" on the second floor.

So Mark turned to the right and hurried as best he could along the hall, walking on the balls of his bare feet to make as little noise as possible. He trailed the fingers of his left hand along the wall to keep himself oriented as he moved toward what he hoped was a way out. He had no other thought beyond escape. His breath was hot in his throat. He could do this. He was almost there. He would get out of this horrible place and flag down a car or run to a house and ask to use the phone, call the police—call *Pearce*—and then this nightmare would be over. He would be safe.

The girls inside this place would be safe. These men would be in jail.

The hallway ended at the dirty double-hung window. There were no back stairs, no other way out. Mark flipped open the lock on the window and tried to pull it up, but it wouldn't budge. He tried again, stifling a grunt of exertion, feeling his pulse throb in the sensitive spot on the back of his head.

"He's there!"

The shout from behind pushed him into panic mode. He pulled his hands back and then thrust them forward, banging his palms against the window, shattering the glass. Footsteps pounded closer behind him as he shoved his head out into the fresh air and dazzling sunlight. A short span of roof sloped away from beneath the window, and he put his hands on the sill, ignoring the sharp bite from the jagged glass still stuck in the frame. The roof shingles were hot from the sun and burned his bare shoulder as he rolled out the window. The slope of the roof was steep enough for him to lose control of his roll, and he couldn't help screaming as he tumbled off the edge into space, the men shouting from the window above him.

Mark landed on his side and felt the air leave him in a rush. He choked and tried to gasp in breath, but his lungs didn't seem to remember how to work. There was no time for him to recover, however, and he rolled over onto all fours. Pebbles and stones ground into his lacerated palms and scraped up his knees, but he pushed the pain to the back of his mind. Right now he needed to escape, to live. He got to his feet and stumbled away from what he now realized was a house, running blind as blood dripped from his palms and splattered his legs. He didn't look back; he focused his blurred vision on cars driving past an opening in the chain-link fence that surrounded the house.

He was so close. Mark could almost feel Pearce's arms around him, hear Pearce's voice as he whispered that Mark was safe, that everything would be all right. Not long now. Just a little farther, and he would be out in traffic. Surely someone would stop; someone would call the police.

A car slowed to a stop on the street just outside the gap in the fence, its lines a red blur without his glasses, and Mark's heart stuttered. This was it; he was saved. This driver would see him running toward him, nude and bleeding, and call the police. He opened his mouth to scream, to call for help, but his lungs still weren't pulling in enough air after the fall from the roof, and no words came out.

With five yards to go, Mark lifted his arms over his head and waved them back and forth. His words were hoarse shouts, and he felt drops of blood from his palms land on his face. The blurred red car pulled away, and Mark's hope went with it. His chest was tight and hot, and he could no longer get his breath. He pushed himself toward the opening, forced his bare feet to move one more step, and then one more after that, all the while waiting to hear a gunshot from behind him, feel the hot punch of the bullet hitting him in the back.

More cars drove past the opening in the fence, and Mark managed to get out one loud shout of "Help!" before someone tackled him from behind. He went down hard, dirt and rocks scraping against his wounded palms. His cock and balls raked across the ground as well. At the last moment he turned his head to the side and avoid hitting face-first but felt his left cheek burn as it rubbed against the loose stones.

The hard barrel of a gun was jabbed against the base of his skull, and a man with horrible breath whispered in his ear, "I don't care how many cars are driving past. I will shoot you right here and then go inside and rape every one of those girls before I put a bullet in each of their heads as well if you do not stand up and go back to the house. Is that clear?"

A hard, worn-out sob burned in Mark's throat as he nodded.

"Good. Now get up and move."

His muscles shook, and every part of him hurt as Mark got to his feet. The tears in his eyes sharpened his sight for a quick moment, allowing him to see the cars moving past on the road just beyond the break in the fence. Beyond the road, he saw palm trees standing tall, their fronds waving in the ocean breeze.

"Don't even think about it," the man behind him grumbled, pressing the gun against the small of Mark's back. "If I shoot you in the spine, you would most likely live but be paralyzed, and we could still sell you to someone with that kind of fetish."

"Fucking animal," Mark said, his voice a whisper.

"That's right," the man agreed. "And like an animal, I have no compassion either. Move."

Mark turned away from the break in the fence to see five men standing between him and the house, all of them glaring at him and holding an assortment of weapons. With tears running down his dirty, scraped cheek, Mark limped slowly back toward the house.

CHAPTER 13

Pearce eased the black T-shirt over his head just as Detective Arnott stepped into his hospital room. "Any word on Mark?"

"I'm sorry, no, Mr. Pearce. Are you ready to be released?"

Pearce nodded. "Definitely." He sat in the plastic chair and slowly bent over to pull on his shoes. He closed his eyes against the sudden pulse of a headache before sitting upright and turning to the detective. "Concussions are always easier to get over in books and movies."

"I have not been in a position to know myself." Arnott crossed the room to look out the window at the street below. "While you have been here in hospital, I had the need to gain access to your room to retrieve your identification and insurance information for the hospital's records. I had Isaiah, the head of security, open your room's safe so I could obtain your wallet. I hope you do not mind."

Pearce felt a quiver of nervousness, but he smiled as best he could and said, "No, it's all right. I appreciate that."

"While I was leaving the room, I had the chance to speak to some of the guests who were staying in the rooms around yours."

"Oh?" Pearce felt his hands gripping the smooth plastic edges of the chair's seat beneath him and forced his fingers to relax, moving them to rest on his thighs instead. "And what did you learn? That Mark and I were quiet neighbors and didn't argue or shout at each other or break things?"

Arnott turned and smiled. "They had nothing to say about your habits in the room, you are correct. But there was a couple who recalled seeing the two of you have some sort of disagreement the day Mark disappeared."

Pearce sighed and closed his eyes a moment, frustration and outrage twisting within him like a long string of barbed wire. He got to his feet, swayed briefly at the light-headedness, and then glared at Arnott. "I already told you we had an argument. That wasn't a secret, and it was the reason Mark went off on his own, back to the Bridgetown Bar where he got into trouble. That's where I found his flip-flop, right by the Dumpster, just before I was attacked."

Arnott nodded, turned to face him again, and leaned back against the windowsill, crossing his arms. "Yes, this is true. But we have inspected the area behind the Bridgetown Bar very thoroughly in the daylight and found no flip-flops or any other evidence of Mr. Beecher having been there."

"Well, what about the fact that someone beat the crap out of me and put me in the hospital? Doesn't that give you an idea that something's not right about that bar?"

"Abraham still claims to have no knowledge of an attack behind his establishment two nights ago, and his alibis still stand by their statements that he was inside the bar the entire time. You were lurking behind the bar late at night, and it is located off the normal tourist path. I have nothing on which to base a charge for Abraham, Mr. Pearce. Surely as a man of the law back in the States, you can understand my position."

"Yeah, I understand it, all right," Pearce grumbled. He pulled open the door to stomp out into the hall, nearly knocking over a nurse in the process.

"You need to be discharged," the nurse said. "You can't just walk out like this."

"Then let's get it going," Pearce snapped. "I have to get out of here."

"Go back into your room and have a seat, Mr. Pearce," the nurse instructed. "I'll have the paperwork in to you in a few moments."

"Send it to my hotel, and I'll sign there." Pearce turned toward the elevator. Behind him he heard Arnott's frustratingly calm and even voice tell the nurse it was okay to let him go, that Arnott would see Pearce got to his hotel and signed the paperwork there. Pearce wanted to punch the detective in the face but figured that would just get him thrown in jail and keep him from looking for Mark for yet another night, at the least.

He jabbed the elevator button and shook his head, flinching at the pain that buzzed up the back of his neck. Didn't they hand out pain medication here on the island? Oh, right, he probably would have gotten a prescription if he'd signed the discharge papers like a normal person. Well, fuck that. He needed to get back to the Bridgetown Bar and check even more thoroughly around that Dumpster. Or maybe find out where Abraham lived and check out his residence.

Arnott walked up to stand beside him just as the elevator doors opened. "You are giving Americans a bad name on our island."

"Your island is giving Rihanna a bad name," Pearce said and stepped into the elevator car, Arnott right behind him. Three other people stood in the car, gazes locked on the numbers above the doors.

They rode to the lobby in silence, and when Pearce stepped out of the elevator, he turned to walk off down the hall.

"Mr. Pearce?" Arnott called to him, but he ignored the man and kept walking. He'd find a taxi to take him to the hotel.

"You're going the wrong way, Mr. Pearce."

Pearce stopped and looked at the signs painted on the wall. Sure enough, PARKING and EXIT had arrows pointed back toward the elevator.

"Fuck," Pearce said beneath his breath and reluctantly turned to walk back to where the detective stood grinning.

"I will give you a ride back to your hotel," Arnott said.

"No need. I'll get a cab."

"I insist." Arnott waved for Pearce to walk ahead of him.

"Fine."

Pearce headed toward the door, quietly satisfied to hear Arnott say from behind him, "And you're welcome."

The drive to the hotel was short and silent, for which Pearce was thankful. He kept his eyes closed and his head back against the seat the entire time. When Arnott stepped out of the car to follow him into the hotel, Pearce extended his hand to the detective.

"You've gone out of your way for me, and I thank you," he said. "But I can make it up to my room all right now."

"What kind of detective would I be if I didn't see the victim of a crime safely back to his room?" Arnott asked. "Come, let's go inside."

Pearce rolled his eyes, making sure the detective saw him do it, then turned to step into the hotel. They were silent during the elevator ride up to the fifth floor. Pearce knew how this was going to play out. Arnott was going to enter the room with him, saying it was just to be sure he got in all right. Then he was going to bring up something he might have noticed while he was looking for Pearce's wallet, maybe ask to see Mark's spare glasses, his cell phone, or his wallet once more. Arnott most likely would ask which places in Barbados he and Mark had visited and then suggest that maybe searches should be conducted of the caves and remote places they had explored, just as a precaution, of course, in case the worst had happened and Mark's body would be found there. Or maybe Pearce and Mark had argued when they'd been out on their own, and maybe after the disagreement in the dining room, things had escalated fast, as sometimes happens when emotions and tempers are high.

This was how suspects felt, Pearce realized as he used his key card to open the door to the room. Arnott followed him inside. Pearce had been in Arnott's position more times than he could count, questioning people and trying to decipher the truth from the lies, but he hadn't spent time as a suspect. He'd been in trouble enough—plenty of times, actually—with Assistant Director Harris back home in the office, but not a suspect. And never outside the United States.

A heavy pulse of pain beat in the back of Pearce's head, and he excused himself to use the bathroom. He closed the door behind him and sat on the toilet seat with his head in his hands. He needed to focus, get Arnott to focus, so they could find Mark and bring him back. Pearce knew the Bridgetown Bar had something to do with Mark's disappearance, but he was at a standstill when he tried to figure out where Mark was being held. It was very possible Mark was dead, killed for seeing something, for stumbling on a crime in progress or figuring out the truth about the girl on the porch.

Regret, hot and acidic, burned in Pearce's gut. He should have listened more closely to Mark, made more of an effort. But after the events at the Speaker of the House's party, Pearce figured they had both needed to relax and stay out of another mystery. And look where that had gotten them.

He couldn't lose Mark, not like this. Not ever. Mark grounded him in a way no other man seemed capable of. He knew when to let things ride and when to call Pearce out on his bullshit, and he understood how Pearce thought, how his job as an agent defined him more than he liked to admit.

It was cheesy as hell, but Mark made him whole.

"Are you all right in there, Mr. Pearce?" Arnott asked through the door.

Pearce lifted his head and grimaced at the pain. "Just fine, Mom, thanks. Be out in a minute."

"Take your time, of course," Arnott responded. "I'll just make myself at home out here."

That got Pearce's attention, as Arnott had known it would, and he stood up and turned to the mirror, surprised when he caught sight of his reflection. He looked like shit. Hell, he looked like the shit that shit crapped out. One of his eyes was blackened, butterfly bandages kept a cut on his temple together, and blood had dried to the skin of his forehead.

He dug into his shaving kit for some painkillers and swallowed four of them with a cup of water. He then ran the water until it was warm and splashed it on his face, then gently ran his hands through his hair. A blaze of pain sent him to one knee and gasping for breath. He closed his eyes and fought back the churning nausea. He won this round, but just barely. The bland meal he'd eaten in the hospital stayed in his belly, and he slowly got to his feet. He splashed more water on his face, rinsed his mouth, and then brushed his teeth. Finally he patted dry his face and stepped out of the bathroom to find Arnott sifting through the clothes in the top drawer of the dresser.

"Yeah, sure, go ahead and paw through our stuff," Pearce said, his voice a low growl. "Shouldn't you be out trying to find Mark?"

"The RBPF officers know he is missing." Arnott slid the drawer shut. "I do need to ask you a few more questions, if you feel up for it."

Pearce cocked an eyebrow. "Do I have a choice?"

Arnott smiled. "I like you, Mr. Pearce. Under other circumstances, we might enjoy each other's company."

"I'm flattered." Pearce waved his hand in a circular motion. "Let's get this over with. We're wasting time."

"These are the standard questions I need to ask," Arnott said. "You know this is true."

"Yep. Absolutely. Ask away."

"Mr. Beecher's wallet and mobile phone are still here, you said?"

"Yeah, they're in the safe here," Pearce said. "I'm sure you saw them when you got my wallet."

"Perhaps," Arnott replied. "But could you show me again? We had to set a new combination, since the safe was opened with the master code."

Pearce opened the closet and got down on his knees before the safe. He punched in the code the detective relayed and then reached in to extract the items.

Arnott looked at the picture on Mark's license and checked how much cash was left. He opened the hard shell case and withdrew Mark's spare glasses, then turned the smartphone over in his hand. "This has been powered off the whole time you have been here?"

Pearce nodded. "Yeah. Yes. We don't have international service."

"I see." Arnott fixed his gaze on Pearce, watchful, steady, unnerving. "Difficult to keep track of each other after being used to text messages and voice mail."

"Yes, it is."

"Did he leave a note here in the room?" Arnott turned away, and Pearce took advantage of the opportunity to lift a trembling hand to his forehead and wipe away the beads of sweat that had formed there. He didn't know if it was from nerves or the concussion, but he didn't like it.

"No, I looked for a note. I have looked several times, but I haven't found one." Pearce cleared his throat. "You said you've checked behind the Bridgetown Bar, but what about along the side of the road leading to the city itself?"

"Yes, we did that as well. Last night and this morning. We found nothing but a dead stray dog." Arnott turned to face him, Mark's mobile phone still in his hand. "So you argued, you said, about the girl at the bar. Were you jealous?"

"What? No!" Pearce rolled his eyes and then immediately regretted it as an ache thundered through his head. "Look, I was ticked off because he said he would let it go after we went back and talked to the bartender, and he didn't. That's all. I wasn't jealous, and he isn't attracted to women. Neither of us is. He was just reminded of a girl back in high school who disappeared while on her senior trip."

"And why did you not come to the RBPF to report Mr. Beecher's suspicions?"

"Because, Arnott, we had nothing to base them on but a person Mark remembered from back in high school, okay?" He put a hand he was surprised to see tremble to his forehead again. "It's been a really bad couple of days. Can we not do this right now?"

Arnott gave him a chilly smile. "Very well, Mr. Pearce. I understand you need some rest. Oh, which reminds me, the nurse handed me this prescription for a strong painkiller. Shall I leave it at the front desk to be filled?"

"That would be good, thanks," Pearce said.

With a nod, Arnott stepped past Pearce toward the door but then stopped and turned around, Mark's wallet still in his hand. "One more thing, Mr. Pearce. Do you have a recent photo of Mr. Beecher I could hand out to the RBPF officers? They could show the picture to people on the street when they ask whether Mr. Beecher has been seen." He lifted Mark's wallet. "Or may I keep Mr. Beecher's driver license for a time to make a copy of the picture?"

There was no way Pearce was going to let the man walk off with

Mark's driver license, RBPF detective or not. He reached out for the wallet and said, "I'd prefer you use one of the digital photos we took earlier in the trip."

"Ah, very good. A more recent picture would, of course, be best."

Pearce crossed the room to where he had plugged in the digital camera and scrolled through the pictures on the camera's memory disc. A smile, small and sad, touched his lips as he browsed through the pictures they had taken around the various tourist spots. Mark had surreptitiously snapped a few pictures of Pearce sleeping nude in the room, his cock hard as he lay sprawled on his back, mouth opened and one arm crooked over his head, and he hurriedly scanned past those.

Maybe this had been a bad suggestion.

He squinted through the dull headache and said, "I'd like to hang on to the camera, though. Can I check with the desk later when I go downstairs and see if they have a printer that will accept the memory card, have it e-mailed to you? Will that work?"

Arnott fixed him with a long, assessing stare. Finally, he nodded and tipped his head toward the door. "I'll be leaving, then. But I'll check in with you tomorrow. May I suggest you stay in your hotel room tonight, Mr. Pearce, and leave the investigation to us?"

"Yeah, sure," Pearce said with a sheepish smile. "I think I've learned my lesson."

"I should hope so." Arnott checked his watch. "It is six o'clock. You still have time for dinner in the hotel dining room."

"That and a good, long sleep are on my list," Pearce said while thinking, *Not to mention following Abraham after he closes the bar.* "Thank you again, Detective."

Arnott held Pearce's gaze a long moment, nodded, then said as he turned to open the door, "Get some sleep. Your prescription will be waiting for you at the desk."

Once the door had shut behind Arnott, Pearce waited fifteen

minutes and then headed to the elevator. In the lobby, he made sure Arnott wasn't lingering anywhere, watching for him, and then went out by the freshwater pool. He squinted against the setting sun, the bright light like a spike directly into the sore spot on his skull, and cursed himself for not bringing his sunglasses. Pearce shaded his eyes and made his way to the scooter rental booth, where he had to wait while two young women checked out scooters. They giggled and joked about driving into palm trees, and Pearce quietly wished them safely back to the hotel later as they puttered off along the asphalt path and down the driveway.

He checked out a scooter, a red Vespa with a disconcerting scrape along the fuel tank, paid extra for a lock and chain, and after gunning the throttle, rode the bike down the asphalt path. At the driveway, he turned toward the main entrance, then wove around taxis and guests coming and going as he aimed for a small, shaded lot where he had seen hotel employees park their personal scooters. He parked his rental near a brightly painted bike rack, chained up the scooter, then pocketed the key as he stepped inside the hotel's main entrance.

Back in the room, he stumbled to the bed, slowly peeling off items of clothing. He needed to rest for a few hours—there was no doubt in his mind about that—but not for long. Mark needed him, and Pearce needed to get Mark back. He couldn't even try to imagine what was happening to Mark right now. All Pearce could focus on was finding him and taking him home.

CHAPTER 14

Mark was being carried.

His left arm ached. More than ached; it hurt like hell, the pain radiating out from the crook in his elbow and up and down his arm. They had dressed him again in his shirt and shorts, but he was still barefoot. He moaned and moved his legs and arms, but the men carrying him, one holding his legs and the other his arms, only tightened their grips and continued walking.

Mark floated within the haze of whatever drug they had been giving him, but he tried to stay alert, to make himself focus on his surroundings. If he could get away, get to a phone and call the hotel or call the police, he could tell someone he was still alive. Maybe they could trace the call or would know from caller ID or something where he was located.

Did Barbados have caller ID? Didn't every phone system in the world have it by now?

He grunted as his left elbow struck something and pain shot up his arm and into his shoulder. One of the men carrying him grumbled, "Careful. No further cuts or bruises, or they lower the payment."

Mark drifted.

When he came back around, he was in a car that was driving fast. All around him, Mark heard the sounds of traffic—cars, trucks, and scooters—and he moaned quietly, trying to make a sound of his own, trying to be noticed.

"He's awake again," a man said, his voice low and deep, like an avalanche in Mark's ears.

"Can't give him any more," another man said, his voice much higher than the first man's. "He's a fighter, I'll say that."

"They'll beat that out of him in a few weeks," Deep-voice said and laughed.

Mark forced his dry lips apart and let out a quiet, raspy word: "Help."

"Shit. Now he's talking?" High-voice said with a disgusted tone.

"Told you," Deep-voice rumbled. "Should have given him another dose before we loaded him into the car."

"I can't give it to him now," High-voice said. "Not with your driving."

The car swerved, slaloming from one side of the road to the other. Mark was laying face up on the backseat and reached out a hand to steady himself against the back of the front seat. His cut palm touched the rough fabric and he cried out. More laughter from the men up front. Mark opened his eyes and squinted against the glare of sunlight. Through the window near his feet, he saw blue sky and palm trees speeding past.

"We'll be at the boat soon," Deep-voice said. "You can give him the shot once he's on board."

A cold tremble of panic started up in Mark's belly. He was being taken to a boat? If they put him on a boat, he knew he'd disappear forever. He had to try to stay on the island, to stay where Pearce would be searching for him. He had to fight to stay close to Pearce.

With even more effort than it had taken to open his eyes, Mark pulled one leg up and kicked out, connecting with the door. It thumped beneath his bare foot, and he heard the high-voiced man let out a squeak of surprise. Mark kicked again, harder this time, clenching his teeth together. His foot connected with the door, and it rattled in the frame.

The car swerved, and the driver shouted, "What the fuck?"

"He's kicking the fucking door!" High-voice shrieked. "Drive faster!"

"In case you haven't noticed, there's a lot of traffic on this road."

Mark kicked the door again, and once more it rattled in the frame. Then he shifted his aim and slammed his foot against the window glass. It trembled from the blow, and he pulled back his leg another time only to feel someone grab hold of it. It was High-voice, leaning over from the front seat and gripping Mark's leg tight to keep him from kicking again.

Bringing his hands into the fight, Mark slapped and scratched at the man, ignoring the painful cuts on his palms. He dug his nails into the skin of the man's face and was rewarded with a shriek of pain and the release of his leg.

"He fucking scratched me!" the man shouted.

Mark struck out with his foot again and again. The window cracked and splintered. He pulled back his leg for another kick, but the driver hit the brakes—hard—and Mark tumbled into the footwell of the backseat. Pain burned along his left arm, making him dizzy.

"Now get back there and dose him again," the deep-voiced driver said.

Mark felt someone crawl over him from the front seat into the back. He tried to kick and scratch, but he was in no position to strike out. His left arm was seized and bent back at an awkward angle, and Mark cried out. A sharp sting in his skin, and then a heavy, warm feeling rushed over him, relaxing him and taking him under once again.

———

THE ALARM on the clock radio went off at nine p.m., dragging Pearce out of a deep, dreamless sleep. He hit the Snooze button and when the alarm went off a second time, hauled himself out of bed and into the bathroom. The shower felt like needles on the tender spot on the back of his skull, and he gently worked shampoo into his hair, watching the bits of dirt and dried blood wash away toward the drain.

He felt better after he'd showered, a little more alert, and he dressed in a black polo and khaki cargo shorts with tennis shoes. Leaving his wallet on the dresser once more, just in case Arnott needed to get his ID again, Pearce stuck some cash in his pocket and headed out the door.

As Arnott had promised, his prescription painkillers were waiting at the front desk. He read the label—take with food, of fucking course—and then asked the young woman behind the desk where he might get something to eat.

"Hijinks is open, and they serve food from the kitchen," she replied, pointing toward the door that led out to the pool.

"Hijinks?"

"The bar just by the freshwater pool. Right through that door."

"Oh, I didn't know that place had a name," Pearce replied. "I've just been calling it the bar by the pool."

"That works as well, sir," she said and flashed him a bright, patient smile.

"Thanks." He started to turn away, then remembered Arnott had wanted a picture of Mark and turned back. "Sorry. One more question. Do you have a printer I can use that's able to send an e-mail of a photo from an SD disc?"

"I don't know about the capabilities of the printers, but the business center is just around the corner here, with computers and printers available for guests to use." She gestured to a hallway to the right.

In the business center, Pearce found a printer that accepted the type of memory card used by his digital camera. He slipped the card into the slot and scrolled through the images, a hot stone of regret and fear settling in him at the fun they had been having before all this shit happened. Damn it, he should have listened to Mark, really listened to him. Realized how important the situation was to him and done more to stop it. Coulda, shoulda, woulda, Pearce thought. Time to stop looking back, thinking he should have handled something better, and look at what was right in front of him and act like Mark mattered.

As he scrolled through the photos, Pearce came on a close-up he had snapped of Mark in the Flower Forest, and he stopped. This was a good picture for Arnott to use. He pulled the detective's business card from his pocket and punched in the e-mail address. He also printed off several color copies he could use when he asked people about Mark.

He stopped at the front desk again and asked for two envelopes, then wrote Mark's name on the back of two copies of his picture, folded them, and put one in each envelope. He wrote Arnott's name on one and Isaiah from hotel security on the other before handing them back over the desk. With his own copy folded and resting in his pocket beside the bottle of painkillers, Pearce headed out the door to the bar.

The reggae music was loud, and Pearce squinted against a headache. He kept his distance from the bar lined with loud, happy, drunk hotel guests and a variety of hangers-on, opting instead for a table in a back corner with no speaker above it. A breeze off the water felt good, and when the waitress came up, he ordered a burger and fries and, since he would be taking painkillers, a diet soda instead of the beer he really wanted to have.

"Bring it right up," she said and walked off.

Pearce stared out over the beach at the moonlit water, remembering their first day at the hotel, when they had spent the entire afternoon side by side on loungers, soaking up the sun. Mark's wrist cast had been removed the day before they'd left, and the skin had been very pale. They'd joked about it, Pearce suggesting some extra sunscreen and maybe that Mark should have stuck his arm in a tanning bed to even things out. The memory of that day made him smile.

The bright, high-pitched laughter of two girls pulled Pearce from his thoughts, and he looked toward the bar. Two young blonde girls stood sipping drinks and talking with an equally young Bajan man. He seemed familiar, but Pearce couldn't place him until he turned his head and smiled, and then recognition clicked. It was the kid who worked the omelet station—the smile clinched it.

Pearce smirked and turned back to the ocean. Growing up on this island must be an odd combination of good and bad: lots of new girls to meet and flirt with, but a small island with limited options for work and relationships.

His food arrived, and Pearce dug in, suddenly hungrier than he had realized. Before he knew it, the burger was gone, and he was left with the fries. They were soggy, but his body craved carbs, and he chewed through them quickly. The movement of his jaw had put pressure on the sore spot on the back of his head, and it now throbbed in time with the reggae music. With the last of his diet soda, he swallowed one pain pill, determined not to take more than that to keep his focus from getting fuzzy. He had to be able to steer the scooter.

Pearce paid for his meal and left a generous tip, then walked past the omelet chef and his two admirers, hearing the young man say, "Come on, it'll be a fun party. You'll love it."

That was what a vacation was for: parties and fun and relaxation, not kidnapping and beatings and hospital stays. His stomach tightened as he walked around the pool, where a broad-shouldered man swam slow lines from one end back to the other.

The scooter was right where he had left it, and Pearce opened the lock, then dropped the chain into the hard-sided carrier. He thumbed the ignition, and the engine turned over, the bike vibrating beneath him. He was glad he'd popped a pain pill, as it had taken the edge off his headache, and he shifted into gear and headed toward Bridgetown.

He followed the yellow beam of the scooter's headlight along the dark, winding road, his senses alert for anything that might rush out of the night beside him or oncoming cars drifting over the center line. The night breeze felt good on his face, keeping him alert, and when he reached the Bridgetown Bar, it was just after eleven o'clock, and the white-gravel parking lot was full. Pearce found a shadowy spot across the street between two businesses closed for the night and backed the scooter in. Recalling the beating he'd received two nights ago, Pearce took the chain out of the storage carrier and wrapped one end around his hand.

With his gaze locked on the bar across the street, he settled in to wait.

At one a.m., Pearce watched the last of the customers, laughing, stumble out the door of the Bridgetown Bar and fall into an older-model European car. The tires threw gravel as the driver hit the gas on his way out of the lot, and Pearce was relieved he wasn't going to be on the road with them anytime soon. There was one car left near the back of the lot, an '80s Cadillac, and Pearce figured it had to belong to Abraham.

Thirty minutes later, his guess was proved correct, as Abraham came out the front door and turned to lock up. The man eased down the short steps and walked slowly toward the car. When Abraham pulled out of the lot, Pearce dropped the chain back into the storage compartment and started the scooter. He let Abraham get a few blocks down the road before he pulled out to follow.

The houses were built closer together in the neighborhood Abraham led Pearce through, tiny cinder block structures built on the cheap to withstand tropical storms. Finally Abraham turned in to the driveway of a small house sandwiched in the middle of a block of similar structures. Pearce pulled to the curb down the street and cut the engine and headlight, then sat straddling the scooter as he watched Abraham let himself in the front door and switch on lights inside.

It was like any working-class neighborhood back in the States. Small houses, some kept up well, others a little more worn down. Nothing at all that would make Pearce think a sex slavery ring was being run out of the place.

"Damn it," Pearce said to himself. His headache was coming back full steam, and exhaustion lurked just behind it. But he couldn't give up now. He had to find Mark, and he knew Abraham was the key.

But what now? From the looks of the house, it had no basement and only two bedrooms, three at the most. Could Mark be tied up in one of the bedrooms? Or in a closet? How the hell was he going to get inside to find out?

Before he could decide on a course of action, the front door of the house opened, and Abraham stepped out onto the porch. He'd changed his shirt and carried an ominous-looking black medical bag.

A tingle streaked through Pearce at the sight of that bag, pulling behind it a cold feeling of dread. What did Abraham carry inside that bag? How many times had he used it on Mark? On young girls taken from their families and friends? The dread curdled into a hardened anger, and Pearce backed the scooter up a driveway into the shadows between two houses to wait, hoping the owners didn't have dogs. He watched Abraham get into his car and back out of the driveway, then turn to head back the way he had come, driving right past Pearce. The light of the dashboard was bright enough that Pearce could see Abraham staring straight ahead, one hand on the wheel.

Pearce pulled out onto the road and followed at what he hoped was a safe distance. He knew he should contact Detective Arnott, but he didn't have time to stop at a pay phone, fearing he'd lose Abraham. Besides, he had no change to make a call. He'd have to follow the man to his next destination and then figure out what to do next.

Traffic was light this time of night, and Pearce had no trouble keeping up with Abraham. The city was dark around them, businesses and homes closed against the night. A few people on the sidewalks, mostly drunks on their way home, called out to him, but Pearce ignored them, keeping his attention on the taillights of Abraham's Cadillac a few blocks ahead.

Minutes later, Abraham's brake lights lit up, prompting Pearce to squeeze the hand brake hard. The scooter's rear tire stuttered to a stop, and Pearce sat astride the idling bike, his heart pounding as he watched the Cadillac turn in to a narrow driveway between two industrial-type buildings.

Was this where they were holding Mark? Both buildings appeared to be abandoned, and it made Pearce almost physically ill to think of Mark inside a place like that, tied up, terrified, possibly injured. Or worse.

There was no other way to see than for Pearce to move closer. He looked around for somewhere to lock up the scooter and settled for a small palm tree nearby, its fronds rustling in the ocean breeze. After securing the chain around the scooter and tree, Pearce cautiously made his way down the sidewalk and, just before the driveway, pressed his back against the building. Music, heavy and thumping, rattled the windows of one of the buildings, and he figured it was some kind of after-hours club. But would they have Mark locked up somewhere inside?

He eased his head around the corner of the building to peer along the driveway. It was heavily shadowed and, as far as he could tell, empty of cars and people. He stepped into the gloom and headed toward the other end, where he could see it opened into an area lined with cars parked in neat rows.

Headlights washed over the walls behind him, startling him, and Pearce ducked his head and ran as the approaching car drove fast along the alley. He had just managed to dart to safety around the corner of the building when the car sped past and turned to the left, away from him, and then circled the crowded parking lot for an open space.

Pearce caught his breath and took in the scene before him. Two big bodyguards sat outside a single entrance, and a line of people stretched out along the back of the building. Some of the people waiting in line swayed and danced to the beat, while others talked and laughed and drank from bottles they hid in purses or sport coats.

It was definitely an underground club, and Pearce wondered if the RBPF knew about it but decided to leave it alone. So long as no one was shot or stabbed, it gave the hard partyers a place to blow off steam away from the tourist-stuffed hotels, so they looked the other way.

Then Pearce noticed Abraham's Cadillac idling quietly in an aisle between parked cars, pointed right toward the entrance of the club. Pearce moved quickly to hide behind the nearest car, almost positive

Abraham had not seen him. If the man had and recognized him, Pearce was pretty sure Abraham would either run him down or shoot him.

A couple staggered out of the club, the girl so drunk her head hung down, and her blonde hair swayed with her erratic movements. Her wobbly steps pulled her date off balance as well, and they both bounced off one of the bodyguards. The big man said something Pearce couldn't make out, and the girl's date, a slender Bajan man, seemed to be apologizing as he walked the girl out into the parking lot.

And that was when Abraham's Cadillac glided silently forward to meet them, like a shark prowling the night.

The man holding his date upright stood and waited for the Cadillac to pull up before him, then reached out to open the back passenger door. He dropped the blonde girl into the backseat, folded her legs in, and then got into the front passenger seat.

Before he closed the car door, the slender man turned to speak to Abraham, and the overhead dome light revealed his features. Pearce's gut wrung itself into a frigid knot as he recognized Salvador, the kid who worked the omelet station at the hotel.

And then it all became clear as he watched the Cadillac roll slowly past his hiding place and down the driveway. Salvador was one of Abraham's soldiers, finding young girls at the hotels and chatting them up, getting friendly, buying them drinks, and inviting them to parties. He most likely got one of them away from her friends, maybe danced with her a bit, kissed her, felt her up. He would slip something into the drink he bought for her and then turn her over to Abraham.

Pearce clenched his jaw hard enough to send barbs of pain blazing across the back of his skull. He closed his eyes and braced himself against the car beside him for a moment, willing the pain away, knowing he had no time for it.

When he felt he could stand, he pushed up to his feet and hurried down the alley to the street. A block away, headed toward the ocean, he saw the taillights of Abraham's Cadillac, and Pearce jogged to where he'd left the scooter, then dug into his pocket for the key to the lock.

In moments he was on the road, his vision blurred from either the wind or the pain throbbing inside his head—or his fear for Mark's life. He blinked away the tears and blotted his eyes on the sleeve of his polo as he urged the scooter faster to keep up with Abraham's Cadillac. *Hold on, Mark. I'm coming. I promise you, I'm coming.*

CHAPTER 15

Minutes after he'd left the club behind, a light mist started to fall. It cast a sheen across the road and soaked into Pearce's clothing. He squinted against the drizzle and tightened his grip on the scooter's handlebars as he followed a few blocks behind Abraham's Cadillac. Fatigue seemed to ride the scooter behind Pearce, cold arms wrapped tight around him, trying to convince him to pull over and find somewhere to lie down, anywhere dry, and rest just for a few moments. He could search for Mark later.

Pearce shook his head hard and flinched at the pain the movement produced. A stream of adrenaline followed right afterward, and he felt more alert after that—so much so that he opened the throttle up just a bit more to close the distance between himself and Abraham.

The bike's headlight burned rainbows in the oil-tinged water of a puddle just before the scooter's front tire hit it and then immediately slipped sideways. Pearce grappled with his balance and resisted squeezing the hand brakes hard, pumping them instead and bringing the scooter to a controlled stop. He put his feet down and hung his head a moment, taking deep breaths to calm his heart rate.

When he raised his head, it was just in time to see Abraham's Cadillac turn a corner farther down the street.

"Damn it!" Pearce gunned the Vespa's motor as he released the brake.

He approached the corner where Abraham had turned and eased out into the intersection. The street stretching before him was empty, not a single parked car in sight.

"Fuck, fuck, fuck, fuck, fuck!" Pearce forced his frustration and exhaustion aside. He needed to focus, to think clearly. The breeze had picked up, and the mist started to slant sideways, falling harder and thicker, more of a rain now. He couldn't lose track of Abraham and Salvador, and especially not the girl they had with them. They were going to lead him to Mark. They had to.

Pearce rode down the street, peering right and left into driveways and parking lots, but found no sign of the Cadillac. The buildings on this block were a mix of tiny ranch houses and small businesses, all the windows dark. He rolled slowly along the street, the rain falling harder, his clothes sticking to him like a layer of skin he was trying to shed.

When he reached the sixth intersection without seeing Abraham or his car, Pearce turned and cruised back toward his starting point. The man had either pulled in to a driveway on this street or had taken another of these side streets. And if that was the case, he could be long gone by now, and Pearce might never find Mark again.

No, that was not an option. He would find that car, and he would track down Mark if it took the rest of his life. He would not rest until he knew Mark was safe.

At the third intersection, Pearce came to a stop and put his feet down to balance himself. He looked left and right along the street. This was halfway between where he had been and where he figured Abraham could have driven to while he had been out of Pearce's sight. He decided to risk it and turned right.

This street had more houses than businesses, a mix of single- and two-story structures. Some of the houses had fenced-in yards, and a few even had rows of hedges along the borders of the lawns. As he rolled past the next intersection, a large black dog rushed out of the shadows at him, barking viciously, its coat wet and shiny with rain. Pearce put on a burst of speed and just managed to outrun the dog as it snapped at his bare legs. He checked over his shoulder a few times, watching the animal run after him until it finally tired and then cut off to duck into a shadowy yard.

"Nice fucking neighborhood," Pearce grumbled, then turned to face forward again. As he passed a two-story house on the corner, a break in the chain-link fence surrounding the property allowed him to see Abraham's Cadillac parked in the driveway. The front passenger door was open and the dome light gleamed in the night like a searchlight. The scooter swerved as his arms jerked in surprise, but Pearce managed to stay upright. His heart pounded and he stared at the car as he motored past. When Abraham himself stood up from the passenger side of the car and stared right at him, Pearce nearly let out a startled shout.

Pearce drove farther along the street, glancing back over his shoulder several times. He was afraid he would see the headlights of the Cadillac flash as the car turned out of the driveway to follow him. But no pursuit came. Perhaps because it was so dark and Pearce himself so rain soaked, Abraham had not recognized him. Either way, Pearce was going to need to be extra careful as he checked out the house.

At a corner a few blocks away, Pearce parked the scooter beside a stop sign. He pulled out the chain and secured the scooter to the sign, pocketed the key to the lock, and made his way down the street. No one was out this time of night and in this weather, and fortunately no dogs cared enough to announce his presence with rounds of barking.

Pearce sidled up along the fence and got down low to the ground to poke his head into the opening to the yard. Abraham's car was still there, and lights were on in some of the windows on the first floor of the house. Moving as quickly and quietly as possible, Pearce got into a crouch and edged his way across the driveway and gloomy yard, his shoes splashing through a few puddles. As he headed toward the back of the house, he noticed a second-floor window had cardboard duct taped over it.

Before he could consider the implications of the cardboard, the front door of the house opened, and two men stepped out onto the small cement stoop. Pearce dropped and flattened himself against the open ground, face turned to watch the men just a dozen feet away.

"I've found you three good pieces the last week, and you still haven't paid me." Pearce recognized Salvador's voice and tightened his fists. He must have meant girls when he said "pieces."

"The American man was an accident," said a deep voice, and when the man moved into the light, Pearce could see it was Abraham, and an icy anger washed over him. He wanted to launch himself at the men and beat them to the ground, but that wouldn't get him any closer to saving Mark. Pearce needed to bide his time, find out Mark's condition and if this was where he was being held.

Abraham continued. "You didn't bring him to us."

"You're making good money off him," Salvador said, his statement sending relief through Pearce. Mark was alive. "I befriended him at the hotel. I should get a cut."

"You're a good worker, Salvador," Abraham said to him. "If you don't get greedy, there might be a place here for you."

"I need to pay my rent," Salvador pushed back, his voice almost a whine. "I took those girls out tonight, spiked this one's drink with stuff I bought on my own. I gotta start getting paid more for these pieces I bring you."

"I understand, I understand," Abraham said. "I know you've been working hard to find us good merchandise, and I want you to know I appreciate it. To show my appreciation, I'll give you something extra next week if you go down to the ship and make sure the American and the red-haired girl leave on time."

"How much extra?"

Abraham chuckled, a low and dangerous sound. "First complete the task, and then next week we'll discuss the payment."

Salvador was quiet a moment, and Pearce was afraid he was going to refuse Abraham's offer. How would Pearce find Mark if Salvador didn't lead Pearce there?

"Why can't you call them?" Salvador asked.

"I've tried," Abraham replied. "Omari and Shaun are not answering."

More silence as the rain pattered down on Pearce's back. His head throbbed, and he closed his eyes to keep dirt and water from splashing into them.

"Okay," Salvador finally said, and Pearce let out a quiet, hopeful breath. "But you promised something extra next week."

"Indeed I did," Abraham assured him. "And I will not let you down."

There was a pause in the conversation, and Pearce cautiously peeled open one eye to see what was going on. Salvador stood in the driveway, hands on his hips as he regarded the Cadillac, and then he turned back to Abraham.

"You going to let me drive the Caddy to the dock and check on the boat?"

Abraham let out a loud, hearty laugh. "No, no, no, my boy. There's a Vespa behind the house, all gassed up. It actually belongs to the hotel where you work."

"You stole it?"

"No, the American man was riding it when he showed up at the bar. I just haven't figured out yet what to do with it."

"What do you want me to do with it?" Salvador asked. "Ride it in the rain down to the docks?"

"It's just a light drizzle. You'll be fine. And then take it back to the hotel, and leave it to be found. It will throw that other American bulla off the track as well as that fuck Arnott."

"What if I get caught?"

"Tell them you found it on the side of the road and were returning it. You'll be regarded as a good employee."

Salvador let out a sigh so loud Pearce could hear it over the rain, which, he noticed with relief, was starting to trickle off. "What time will they leave?"

"The fishing boats leave at five o'clock, which is half an hour from now. Our boat leaves at six."

"That's when I need to be at work to set up my station," Salvador said.

"Then you should go behind the house, get on the scooter, and get going down to the docks."

"All right." Salvador tromped down the steps, and Pearce felt a flutter of fear as he thought the man was going to walk right toward him. Instead Salvador followed a dirt path along the side of the house to an area hidden from sight by a tall wooden fence.

Abraham turned to enter the house as Salvador stepped inside the fenced enclosure, and with both men out of sight, Pearce pushed to his feet and ran back to the sidewalk. Every muscle in his body ached from having lain so still on the hard ground in the cold rain. His headache was back with a vengeance, but he didn't dare take another pain pill. He was so close to finding Mark now; just a little longer and this nightmare would be over. Mark was on a boat at the docks. Pearce only had to follow Salvador to find which one and then figure out a way to save him.

He wanted nothing more than to see Mark again, hold him in his arms, wake up in bed beside him and listen to his quiet snores. Tears stung Pearce's eyes as he approached the scooter and reached into his pocket for the key. His hand came up empty, and he felt a zap of fear. Had he lost the keys back in the yard of the house?

The rattle of another Vespa caught his attention, and he turned to see Salvador guide the scooter, the one Mark had been riding when he'd gone missing, out from behind the fence. Salvador was looking the other way down the street, and before he could turn in Pearce's direction, Pearce ducked around the corner out of sight. He stepped behind a thin palm tree and watched as Salvador motored past. The man didn't even glance his way, and Pearce let out the breath he hadn't realized he'd been holding, then slid his hand into the button-flap pocket of his cargo shorts and touched both keys. He had put them in the secured side pocket, not the front pocket.

"Idiot," he scolded himself, then hurried to unlock the scooter and start it up so he could follow Salvador. He knew his loosely conceived plan could be a waste of time. Salvador could very easily just stop and place a cryptic call from a pay phone or give someone a message to relay up the line. But the forward motion of following Salvador made Pearce feel he was at least doing something by actively searching for Mark.

He refused to believe he would leave the island without Mark beside him. He could not even imagine what that would feel like, how empty a loss like that would leave him.

Shaking his head to clear away those dark thoughts, Pearce focused on Salvador's back a little ways ahead of him. He needed to stay alert, get ready to turn off if Salvador looked behind him. No time for him to start daydreaming now.

Pearce was definitely out of his element.

He had followed Salvador into Bridgetown and across Chamberlain Bridge, then along Wharf Road, until they had come to the fishing harbor. The sun was burning just below the horizon, and the fishing boats had already left the harbor, seabirds circling above them, feathered escorts on their journeys out to sea.

When Salvador eased his scooter to a stop, Pearce pulled off to the side of the road behind a parked car. He watched Salvador lock his scooter to a signpost before he hurried off down a shadowy passage between warehouses where the fishing catches were processed.

Leaving his own scooter on its kickstand, Pearce grabbed the chain from the compartment to use as a weapon and trailed Salvador along the waterfront. His muscles were tensed and he was ready to turn his back or duck behind a truck or crate to stay out of sight should the kid turn around. But Salvador was not concerned about being followed; he was focused on completing his mission and then returning the scooter to the hotel.

The smell around Pearce was at times overwhelming, the air thick with the stench of fish, and the burger Pearce had eaten hours ago rolled in his stomach. Dockworkers walked to and fro, talking and laughing, some grumbling about their boss, others about pay. Pearce tried to blend in, tried to act like he knew where he was going, that he belonged there, but all the men were Bajan, and he really stood out as an intruder. Before long, someone was going to ask him what he was doing there and why he held a length of chain wrapped around his fist.

Salvador moved quickly through the maze of warehouses that sat murky in the gray light of morning, and Pearce barely managed to keep up. At the end of a warehouse, Pearce hung back and watched the kid hurry out along one of the docks. Most of the berths were empty, the boats having already set out for sea, but some vessels, mostly pleasure sailboats, swayed gently on either side.

Pearce was close to Mark now; he couldn't let anything go wrong. If Salvador saw him and alerted the men on the boat before Pearce could get there, it would take too much precious time to get a police boat after them. Mark could be handed off by that time and end up far away. Pearce figured the men planned to take Mark and whatever girls they had to trade out to sea a good distance to meet up with another boat or boats, which would then take them to their respective buyers. Fear and tension knotted together inside him. There was no telling what had been done to Mark already, but Pearce knew either way that this had to end right here, today.

He stepped out from between the warehouses and paused to look around. The fishing boats came and went through a narrow opening in a cement breakwater that protected the dock area. Farther down the waterfront to his left was a heliport, and about a half mile to his right loomed a couple of big cruise ships at dock, their sizes staggering. He spared a moment to wish they had gone on a cruise instead, someplace safe from the local dangers they were currently involved in here in Barbados. When he turned his attention back to the dock ahead of him, he caught a glimpse of Salvador dodging left, then right around stacks of nets before dropping out of sight.

"Shit." Pearce jogged across a blacktop access road and then onto the concrete dock itself. He wished once again that he had his gun and fought back a feeling of defenselessness. He had the chain and could still fight. He just couldn't throw a punch with his right arm like he used to.

Clenching his fists, Pearce walked slowly along the dock. He kept an eye out for Salvador as well as any of the men he might recognize from the Bridgetown Bar. And, of course, he kept an eye out for Mark.

CHAPTER 16

Mark came around slowly. He heard the slap of water against a surface, and it brought up thoughts of summers spent with his family in a cottage in northern Michigan, listening to the water lapping against the boat. Was he back up north?

No, something was wrong. His left arm hurt—real bad—and his hands hurt too. A troubling memory of being in danger floated at the edge of his concentration. Had it been a dream?

Footsteps nearby—overhead, really—and the sound of men's voices, one a low rumble and the other higher pitched. At the sound of the voices, an ice-cold feeling of dread filled his chest and flooded through his limbs. He was more alert now thanks to the adrenaline rush of fear, and he opened his eyes. He was in a small room filled with the gray, pale light of early morning and the briny smell of the sea. The men were in a room above him.

Seagulls cried, and Mark slowly rolled his head toward the wall and squinted at the window. It was round, a porthole, and he understood suddenly that he was on a boat. The realization was followed by a chilling horror that drove him into action. He was being taken to the people who had purchased him from Abraham. He had been sold into sex slavery. But the boat's engines weren't running, so it was possibly still at the dock, and if that was the case, he had a chance.

He needed to sit up and he needed to get away from here and off this boat. If he was still on board when the engines started, he didn't think he'd ever get another chance to get free again.

But something was in his arm, something sharp. He turned his head to see a tube leading up to an IV on his left side. The needle had been stuck in at an odd angle, hurting him, making it pretty much impossible to move his left arm. Mark closed his eyes and focused all his energy on lifting his right arm. He pictured it rising, crossing over his body, and pulling the IV from his left arm. Now that he had it pictured in his mind, he forced his muscles to act on his thought.

He tightened his right hand into a fist, pain from the cuts dulled by the drugs, and Mark felt his arm slowly lift from the mattress. It seemed as if someone else were guiding his hand, controlling him like a marionette. In small increments of movement, Mark reached across his chest, his tingling, half-numb fingers sliding up his left arm until they brushed against the IV tube.

Pain shot up his left arm when the needle was jostled, and he felt tears spill down the sides of his face. But he didn't stop, couldn't risk losing consciousness, and he forced his fingers to open, then close, on the tube. He pulled, felt the needle slip free, leaving behind a warm, wet sensation and a sharp sparkle of pain.

He paused to catch his breath. He didn't take too long, though—he couldn't—and when he was ready, he forced himself to sit up. The world spun beneath and around him, like the worst carnival ride ever, and he leaned forward to vomit between his feet.

As his stomach emptied itself, his thoughts came into sharper focus. He was definitely on a boat, in a small stateroom with a single bed built into each of two walls. He pushed to his feet, avoiding the puddle of sick on the floor, and took a deep breath. Someone lay in the bed across from his, hooked up to an IV like he had been, and he stepped unsteadily across the narrow space to lean on the wood frame of the bunk and look down at the figure.

A girl lay on the bed—the auburn-haired girl he had seen back at the house—her eyes closed and her breathing deep. Mark blinked in the brightening daylight and focused on the IV tube running from the bag hanging from a nail in the wall and down to her arm. He licked his dry lips, leaned down close to her arm—so pale, so thin— and slowly reached out to take hold of the IV. He carefully pulled the needle from her skin and left it dangling toward the floor, dripping onto the stained wood of the deck.

The girl lay still before him, sleeping deeply, and he put a clumsy, comforting hand on her shoulder.

"I'll get us help," he whispered, his lips feeling thick and dumb and his voice sounding as if it came from someone standing far away.

He turned his gaze to the short flight of steps that led to the door. Mark set the goal in his mind and took the first wobbly step in that direction.

THERE WERE MORE boats than Pearce had first thought tied up along the dock. So many boats, and all of them with space belowdecks where someone could be held out of sight.

"Fuck," Pearce muttered and risked standing to his full height to peer around. A breeze made his shirttail flap, and the sounds of boats and men working all around him were distracting. He was running out of time; he could feel it. He had to find the boat Salvador had gone aboard.

Even when he found the boat, he wasn't sure how he was going to save Mark if the men on board had guns. What good was his scooter chain going to be against guns? But that was later; first he had to find it.

Pearce started to walk farther out along the dock, not meeting the eyes of any of the men who turned to watch him pass.

"You!"

The single word shouted from behind brought Pearce to a stop. He looked over his shoulder, trying to keep his expression calm and relaxed as he tightened his grip on the chain. Three men approached him, dirty, sweat-stained tank tops exposing muscular arms. Pearce's gut clenched, and he had to force himself to turn fully and face them.

He didn't have time for this.

"I'm trying to find a friend of mine," Pearce said, hoping his tone was light and friendly. "I was supposed to meet him around here, but I've forgotten the name of the boat."

The man in front, most likely the leader of the trio, frowned at him, his gaze ticking down to the chain in Pearce's hand and then back up to his face. "This dock is not for tourists. This is for working men. You're in the wrong place."

Pearce shook his head. "No, no. I was told to come to this dock specifically. Maybe you've seen him? Young kid, name's Salvador. He works at the Caribbean Breeze Hotel."

"We don't like tourists on our docks," the man said, coming to a stop a few feet away from Pearce. If it came to a fight, Pearce knew he would not be able to win it, even with a weapon. All three men were strong and intimidating.

"Hey, guys, I'm just here trying to find my friend, okay?" Pearce said, and suddenly the truth was coming out before he could stop it. "He's been missing a couple of days, and I'm worried about him. I'm afraid they might be trying to take him off the island on a boat."

The trio's leader frowned. "Your friend is a man?"

"Yes. A blond man, American. I'm very worried about him. I believe he's in a lot of trouble."

The man standing just behind the trio leader's left shoulder leaned in close and whispered something. Without taking his eyes off Pearce, the trio leader nodded slightly.

"Can you help me?" Pearce was now concerned that he was speaking with the very men for whom he was searching. He retreated a step, swung his right arm back slightly, and felt the chain bump against his leg. He clenched his left fist, ready to start throwing punches if needed.

At that moment, a quiet cry of "Help!" rose above the sounds of the seagulls and the boats rocking in the waves. Pearce snapped his head around, pain flaring in his head at the sudden movement. He looked from from boat to boat, desperate for a glimpse of who was in distress. Had that been Mark's voice?

Pearce took off at a run along the dock. Behind him, he could hear the heavy footsteps of the men as they followed in pursuit.

MARK SWAYED ON the short flight of steps but kept his balance. He reached out and braced himself on the door that opened onto the boat's deck as his stomach rolled and a sudden, spiking headache forced him to close his eyes. After fighting back the wave of nausea, Mark thought he had won that battle, but then he felt his control slip away. He leaned out over the side of the stairs and threw up what little he had left in his system.

Sweat coated his body in an oily layer, and when he touched the small doorknob, his hand slipped off it several times before he was able to get a good grip. He listened carefully for any sound on the other side of the door, but all was silent. He held the knob with both hands, the simple motion of turning it difficult because of the sweat and cuts on his palms. The twisting motion sent pain shooting up his left arm and brought tears to his eyes.

The door popped open, loud to his ears, and he whispered, "Shh. Quiet. Shh," to the door as if it could hear and understand him. No one shouted; no one came running to stop him. Emboldened, he glanced back at the girl still out of it on the bunk across from his and then pushed the door open and climbed up.

Two men were talking somewhere nearby; Mark could hear their gruff voices. He crawled out from belowdecks and, still on his hands and knees, traveled a short distance from the door. He was in a small cabin, windows all around him. The men were above him, sitting in the wheelhouse, most likely. Boxes stacked on top of one another and covered with plastic provided concealment. As he leaned back against the boxes, the plastic rustled quietly, and Mark sucked in a frightened breath. The men above him fell quiet for a moment.

"You hear that?" the deep-voiced man asked.

"Yeah. The wind moving that fucking plastic, maybe?" suggested the man with the higher voice.

"Yeah, probably," rumbled the first man. "When do we leave, again? We're going to miss our meeting if we don't leave soon."

"I thought Abraham wanted to bring us a couple more girls," said High-voice. "Maybe he wanted one last morning with them."

The men laughed, and Mark closed his eyes and clenched his teeth. He had to get off this boat, had to warn someone about what was going on. Deep breaths helped him clear his head, and he stood up. It took a moment for him to feel ready to walk. He was going to have to move fast to stay away from the men above him. If he was lucky, they were facing the front of the boat—the bow? The stern? He could never remember—and they wouldn't see him until he was already on the dock.

Two shaky steps took him out into the open, the morning

sunlight warm on his skin, and he didn't dare risk stopping. He just needed to get off the boat. He moved as quickly as possible, frustrated with his lack of balance and the softly blurred edges around everything. The deck seemed to pitch and sway beneath his feet, and he stopped, arms out to keep himself steady, eyes closed. He found his center once more and started forward again.

He made it to the narrow board between the boat and the dock, had just grabbed on to the side of the boat for stability, when someone appeared on the dock before him. He squinted and frowned. The man seemed familiar, but his features were blurred from Mark's poor vision and the drugs in his system. How did he know this man? Then it clicked, and he let out a gasp of relief when he recognized Salvador, the kid who manned the omelet station at the hotel.

"Salvador," Mark whispered, waving for the man to ascend the gangplank toward him. "Help me." He checked over his shoulder, but the men had not yet seen him. "They're holding me here. Help me."

"No, no, no," Salvador said, his voice rising in pitch and volume as he walked up the board and took Mark by the shoulders. "You cannot go!"

"No!" Terror, cold and shocking, exploded within Mark, clearing his head and strengthening his muscles and voice. Salvador was part of the gang. Salvador was going to keep him prisoner. But Mark had come too far to back down now. He struggled against Salvador's grip, saying, "I have to leave. I have to get away. Help!" Mark's voice gained power, and he leaned over Salvador's shoulder as if the extra two inches could push his voice farther out across the dock. "Help me! Help!"

Salvador pushed him back across the deck, the two of them standing so close it was like some kind of dance. Mark tried to resist by setting his right leg behind him, stopping his motion for a moment, and pushing back against Salvador, shouting for help the whole time.

Behind him he heard the curses of the men up in the wheelhouse. He felt the rumble of their steps across the deck as they came up behind him. His shouts turned to screams, high-pitched and terrified, and he flailed his limbs in panic as the three men grabbed his arms and dragged him back toward the cabin.

"MARK!" PEARCE SHOUTED, knowing for certain that was Mark's voice, that he was alive and in trouble. "Where are you? It's Aaron!"

"Help!" Mark was screaming now, the terror evident in his voice, and it stabbed into Pearce like a blade.

"Mark!" Pearce shouted again, running faster, swinging his head back and forth, looking from boat to boat, desperate to find him. Where was he? He could hear Mark but couldn't see him.

Then a flash of movement: three men struggling with a man with blond hair. A glimpse of the man's face—the sight of Mark striking out, eyes wide, mouth open as he screamed again—sent a surge of anger twined tightly with hope through Pearce. He heard the three men still behind him and put on speed to stay ahead of them. First he would grab Mark, touch him, feel him in his arms, and then he would find a way to get him away from these thugs and back to safety. Over the side of the boat and into the water if that was what it took.

He reached the boat at full speed and pushed off with one foot, using his right arm to vault over the gunwale. He landed on the deck and quickly assessed the situation. Mark was in the middle of the three men, and Pearce couldn't risk hitting him with the chain. Instead he reached out and grabbed Salvador, snagging his loose-fitting T-shirt. The young kid was skinny and wiry, but Pearce's adrenaline was up, and he pitched him easily toward the rear of the boat.

"Mark!" Pearce shouted, letting Mark know he was there.

"Aaron! Aaron!" Mark cried as the remaining two men managed to pull him toward the boat's cabin.

The three men who had been chasing Pearce clambered onto the boat. Pearce turned and saw their fists clenched, muscles braced for battle. Instead of attacking him, however, the leader of the trio grabbed Salvador by the arm as the kid scrambled to his feet, and handed him off to one of the other two men, saying in a gruff voice, "Hold him."

Relief, cautious and cool, swept through Pearce, and he turned to face the two men holding Mark. His relief burned away as he saw sunlight glitter along the dark metal of a gun that one of the men, the smaller one, stuck into Mark's side.

"Drop the chain, motherfucker," the armed man said.

Pearce held his left hand out, palm up, and let the chain unwind from his right into a gleaming pile on the deck by his foot. "Easy now. I just want my friend. We can all be reasonable."

"Shut the fuck up!" the man shouted.

"Aaron," Mark said, his wide eyes fixed on Pearce, tears streaming down his face. "Please."

"I'm here," Pearce said. "Don't worry. Just like the kitchen back in Washington. Remember?"

Mark stared at him for a long moment, and Pearce was afraid he didn't understand. But then Mark nodded, closed his eyes, and tried to spin out of his captor's grasp, but he was too weak didn't go far. As Mark turned, Pearce saw the dark bruises and blood trailing down his left arm, and a cold hook of pain jabbed into Pearce's heart. Mark had been drugged this whole time and was still woozy from the effects.

Pearce feinted forward, but the man with the gun curled his arm around Mark's neck, holding him in place, and pressed the barrel against Mark's temple.

"Put down the fucking gun. I'm with the FBI. This isn't going to end well for you. It's over. Let him go."

"FBI? You're out of your country," said the man who stood behind his partner. "You can't arrest us."

"I can kill you in self-defense."

"You'll die too, then," the skinny man said in a surprisingly deep voice for his body type.

"Gonna have to take a lot of us out, friend," the leader of the trio said from beside Pearce. "Put down the gun. Let the man go."

Pearce met Mark's gaze, saw how spaced he was, and knew he couldn't depend on Mark to react quickly. The situation was dangerous, but Pearce felt he could get the upper hand with a little help—something—from Mark.

"I'm telling you to let him go!" Pearce shouted and inched closer. "What you're doing is sick and immoral, and you'll never get out of this harbor. Put down the fucking gun and let him go."

The man with the gun shifted his gaze between Pearce and the trio leader. Pearce spared a moment to admire the bravery of the man from the dock. This wasn't his personal battle, but here he stood, facing down a man with a gun.

There was a long moment when Pearce thought the man would put the gun down and it would all be over. But then the expression on his face closed up. He narrowed his eyes and pressed his lips tightly together. He moved the gun, pulling it away from Mark's head to aim at Pearce, rage burning in his eyes.

Mark must have seen the movement out of the corner of his eye. Pearce saw his expression shift to something dark, something harder than he'd ever seen in Mark, just before Mark turned his head and bit hard into his captor's forearm. The man screamed and jerked his arm. The gun went off, and Pearce ducked, but the shot went wide out over the water.

Pearce and his new friend rushed the men at the same time. As the leader of the trio on the dock grappled with the bigger, unarmed man, Pearce wrenched the gun away from the skinny, deep-voiced man. Mark still had his teeth in the man's arm, and Pearce put an arm around Mark's waist and said, "It's Aaron. I've got you. You can let him go."

Mark opened his mouth, and the man staggered backward, then collapsed on his butt in a corner of the cabin while holding his bleeding arm to his chest. "He bit me! He fucking bit me!"

"Aaron?" Mark's mouth had blood all around it, and Pearce used the back of his hand to wipe it away.

"I'm here," he whispered. "I've got you. I'm not going anywhere."

"You found me." Mark had an arm around Pearce's waist and held a fistful of Pearce's shirt as if afraid he'd float away if Pearce released him. "I was so scared. I thought you wouldn't find me."

"It's over," Pearce whispered. "I've got you. You're safe. It's over."

"There are girls at a house," Mark said, tears streaming down his face. "I don't know where it is, but there are more. A lot more. They have to be saved. We've got to save them."

"I know," Pearce assured him. "We'll save them. I know where it is."

"Yeah?" Mark asked, a sob like a hiccup in his throat.

Pearce nodded. "Yeah. Just relax now. You're safe. They're all safe."

"These fuckers are slavers?" asked one of the dockworkers. He had the shirt of the man who had been holding the gun curled tight in his thick fingers.

"Yeah," Pearce replied.

The dockworker turned back and punched the man in the face.

"Fuckin' slavers," said another of the men from the dock. "We should cut them open and dump them in the water for the sharks."

"No!" wheezed the man with the bite mark in his arm and his nose gushing blood. "We're not slavers!"

Another punch to the nose, hard enough to make even Pearce flinch, and the kidnapper sagged in his captor's grip.

The leader of the trio who had approached Pearce on the dock pulled out a mobile phone and dialed a number. Pearce heard him talking to what he assumed was the Royal Barbados Police Force, and he let out a breath. He pulled Mark up against him with his left hand and tightened his grip on the gun in his right.

He'd put the gun down when the RBPF showed up.

He heard the sound of a cruise ship's whistle down at the main dock, and above, the shrieks and screams of seabirds. One of the birds overhead cried loudly, and Mark started in his arms. Pearce hugged him even closer.

"I've got you, Mark," Pearce whispered as Mark cried. "I've got you."

CHAPTER 17

The sheer curtains tied at the supports of the gazebo ruffled in the ocean breeze. Waves mumbled in eternal conversation from the beach at the bottom of the wooden staircase as the fat, orange sun slipped closer to the sea. Mark closed his eyes, soaking in the warmth of the last of the sun.

For the past two days, he'd been out of it, the drugs still in his system, and he was just starting to feel connected to the world again. The two days he'd been held hostage seemed like a dream or some bizarre TV movie he'd stumbled across on cable. Images would flash back to him now and then, snatches of memory rising to the surface of his mind, and he would flinch and have to shake off feelings of fear and panic, his heart pounding and his breath tight. The doctors had assured him that was to be expected after such a harrowing ordeal.

Footsteps on the stairs leading down from the private bungalow startled him upright, and he looked up, then relaxed. It was Aaron, white shirt unbuttoned and flowing behind him in the wind. He carried a bottle of wine and two glasses, and Mark emptied his lungs in a long, steady breath. Things were good. They were together again. He was safe.

"Hey, there," Aaron said as he reached the gazebo. It was built on a platform set halfway between the top of the bluff, where the bungalow was situated, and the private beach below. "Thought we could both use a glass of wine."

Mark smiled at him and nodded, then turned away as tears filled his eyes. There he went again, getting all weepy. How long was it going to take for him to shake off this jittery, jumpy feeling?

"You doing okay?" Aaron asked as he worked with the corkscrew. The cork pulled free with a loud pop. Mark jumped in his seat, then ran a hand across his forehead as a shaky giggle slipped out.

"Mark?" Aaron's voice was deep and concerned.

Mark turned to him, embarrassed at the tear that trickled down his cheek. He wiped it away and nodded. "I'm fine. I am, really. Just jumpy, you know? Having a hard time believing it's over. That this isn't all just a nice dream and I'm still drugged and on that boat."

Pearce opened his arms, glass of wine in one hand and the bottle in the other. "This is no dream. You're here with me, at the far end of the island, in a private bungalow in a securely fenced-in community, upgrade courtesy of the hotel."

Mark snorted and shrugged. "Guess that makes the involvement of their employee okay."

Pearce grunted and set the wineglass before him. "Tomorrow we go back to the RBPF station for final questioning, and then one more day here in our private heaven before we fly out for home."

"Thank God." Mark spun the stem of the wineglass between his fingers. "I can't wait to be back home in our apartment."

Pearce sat beside him and reached out to put his hand on top of Mark's. "Talk to me. What can I do?"

Mark shook his head and smiled. It felt crooked on his face, as if it didn't quite fit, and he knew Pearce would see through his attempt to act carefree. Best to just be honest. "Nothing. I need some time to get over it. Just keep doing what you're doing. Keep being patient with me."

"Come here." Pearce leaned in toward him.

Mark met him halfway for a soft, closed-mouth kiss. At the touch of Pearce's lips, Mark's cock stirred with interest, and a bubble of tension within him burst. He was interested in having sex with Pearce—or making love with Aaron, if he wanted to put it that way. But he had been drugged for most of the time he'd been held, and he had no idea where those needles had come from. The doctor had talked with Mark during his stay in the hospital about the possibility of his having contracted HIV, but Mark had not yet shared that with Pearce. Now it was time.

He pulled back, smiled, then turned his hand over to wrap his fingers around Pearce's and grip his hand, careful of the bandages across his palms. "I want to be with you. I do. But we need to talk about things first."

A frightened expression flashed across Pearce's face, and Mark shook his head. "Don't worry. We're not breaking up."

Pearce nodded, but then his expression shifted to something darker, and he lowered his voice to ask, "Did they...?" He was unable to put into words what he feared had happened.

Mark shook his head again. "No, they didn't rape me. The doctor at the hospital ordered a rape kit to be sure, and everything looked clean. But they did give me shots of Vicodin and hooked me up to an IV, and I have no idea if those needles were clean or had been used before." Mark took a shaky breath and smiled as tears filled his eyes. "I could be infected with HIV, and if that's the case, I don't want to possibly infect you. I could find a way to deal with being infected myself, if it came to that, but if I were to pass it on to you, that would just... I wouldn't be able to live with myself if we didn't take precautions."

Pearce gently took Mark's hand in both of his and stared deep into his eyes. Mark saw the anger and remorse simmering within his gaze. He knew Pearce felt guilty about what had happened, but Mark understood he himself was mostly to blame. Those conversations could wait, however. Right now, he wanted to know Pearce wasn't going to leave.

"Whatever happens, we'll get through it. Together." Pearce leaned in to give him a lingering kiss. "You're not about to get rid of me."

Mark nodded as the tight feeling within his chest loosened just a bit. He hadn't expected Pearce to bolt at the thought of an HIV diagnosis, but thinking something and hearing the man he loved say it were two different things.

Then Pearce surprised him by pushing up from the table to pace the width of the gazebo. He clenched and released his fists as he walked, his unbuttoned shirt showing off his golden-brown skin beneath the dark hair covering his torso. Anger tightened the features of his face and made him look more dangerous – and more handsome – than ever.

"I wish I'd killed them," Pearce said. "They've ruined so many lives."

"We stopped them, though. The RBPF found the three girls from the bar at the house where I was being held, plus a few others. It was Abraham's house, right? It was in his name?"

"Yeah, and he claimed it as a business expense." Pearce shook his head. "Fucker."

"But he's shut down now."

"They caught Abraham at the airport," Pearce grumbled in agreement. "But how many others are waiting to take his place?"

"But we stopped him," Mark said, and he was surprised to hear the optimism in his voice. "And we saved those girls. All those families and friends we helped. *You* helped, actually, by not giving up on me."

Pearce stopped pacing to fix him with an intense look. "I wouldn't have stopped searching, you know. Even if they'd gotten you off the island, I would never have stopped."

A tiny tremble of—what? Intimacy? Passion? Love? Most likely all those things and more combined—worked through Mark. He found he couldn't speak, too choked up on emotion, so he simply nodded instead.

"But how many others before them have dropped out of sight?" Pearce leaned on the railing that surrounded the gazebo and tightly gripped the wood, as if he might be imagining it was Abraham's throat. "How many girls are out there right now? Beaten and raped every day, addicted to drugs because they were forced to take them? All those families back home who are desperate for news, who just want to know what has happened to their daughter or sister or friend." He lowered his head and shook it slowly side to side. "I was so scared you were gone forever. I tried to not believe it, but sometimes it seemed like such a losing battle. And now you have to worry about being HIV positive?" He thumped a fist on the railing. "Fucking bastards."

Mark got up and slipped his arms around Pearce's waist, sighing quietly at the slight tremble he felt when he touched the skin over Pearce's belly. "We'll get through this. I know it was tough for you too."

"Not like it was for you," Pearce mumbled.

Mark kissed his back through the soft cotton of his shirt. "We both went through a lot. But we're back together now, right?"

Pearce turned in Mark's arms to face him and moved in for a kiss. Mark felt the hard length of Pearce's cock press against him, and his own cock responded in kind.

"Together for good," Pearce said, his voice deep with lust. "You're mine."

A thrill shivered up Mark's spine at the words and Pearce's possessive tone. "Oh, I'm yours? That's it?"

Pearce kissed him again, gently tracing the seam of Mark's lips with his tongue, and then said, "I'm yours as well. Body, heart, and soul."

Mark could resist no longer. He pulled Pearce down for a longer kiss, their tongues sweeping together. The doctor at the hospital had assured him that HIV wasn't carried in saliva, and Mark had been relieved that he could still kiss Pearce.

"This okay?" Pearce whispered.

"Yeah. Just...carefully."

"Don't worry." Pearce kissed him before continuing. "We'll play safe. Just want to be with you, come with you."

"Me too. I love you."

"Love you too." Pearce kissed him once more on the mouth and then moved to his throat. The stubble on his jaw scratched Mark's skin, and he groaned. With the sun setting out beyond the sea, the darkening sky above them, and the ocean breeze, Mark thought this might be a place where he could truly begin to heal.

Pearce moved lower, kissed the taut skin of Mark's belly, and then hooked his fingers in the waistband of Mark's shorts and slid them down. Mark sighed as Pearce ran his tongue up and down the sides of his cock. He pressed his mouth against Mark's shaft, then flicked his tongue top to bottom as he moved from tip to root and back.

"Oh shit," Mark said with a gasp. "That's fucking hot."

Pearce leaned back and grinned up at him as he stroked his dick. "I know a thing or two about being safe."

"Guess so." Mark pulled him up for another kiss. He mimicked Pearce's actions and slid down along his torso, parting hair with his tongue and leaving behind a wet trail to cool and dry in the breeze. Pearce's cock twitched and poked at him through his thin cotton pants.

Mark used his teeth to open the bow Pearce had tied in the drawstring and then slid the pants down. He took Pearce's cock deep into his throat, and Pearce let out a loud groan.

"That doesn't seem very fair." Pearce ran his hand through Mark's hair. "You can suck me like that, but I can't do it to you?"

Mark backed off Pearce's cock for a moment. "Enjoy it while it lasts. The day I get a clean bill of health, I'm going to wear your ass out."

"Bring that day on," Pearce said.

Mark resumed sucking Pearce, rolling his tongue around the wide head with each upstroke. He gripped him tightly at the base, fingers pressed into Pearce's bush. He moved faster, tightened his lips around the hot shaft, and was finally rewarded with Pearce's familiar deep grunt. He increased the speed of his sucking even more, moaning as Pearce's cock swelled and hot, thick cum burst into his mouth. He swallowed it down, savoring it, then nursed the last few drops from him before sitting back with a smile.

"You taste good," Mark said.

Pearce returned a dreamy smile and then pulled him to his feet and pushed him back until Mark's bare ass touched the railing. After another kiss, Pearce sat between Mark's legs, both of them with their backs against the rails. He adjusted his position until he was able to take Mark's balls into his mouth, and he reached up to stroke Mark's cock.

"Oh fuck, that feels good." Mark gripped the railing with both hands, then winced a bit at the pain in his palms and the soreness that still lingered in his left arm.

He closed his eyes and focused on the sensations, pushing aside all thoughts about his time being held hostage and turning away from worries about being positive. Pearce was being very safe with him. He let the feeling of Pearce's hand on his cock soothe and excite him and the sensation of his balls in Pearce's mouth push him closer to climax. Nothing mattered right now other than being here, in this private oasis with the man he loved, the man who had worked hard to make sure he had been rescued, the man who would always keep him safe.

In another moment, Mark was right on the edge of his orgasm, and he moaned. Pearce increased the speed of his stroking until Mark toppled over the edge. He cried out as his cock jerked in Pearce's grip, spraying cum across Pearce's legs and the deck of the gazebo.

When he had finished, Mark felt drained, relieved. His ordeal had been shunted to the back of his mind. Maybe he could move on from this experience, not let it haunt him the way Robert Morgan did back home in the States. And maybe he could learn to ease his anxiety about Robert Morgan tracking them down when they got home again.

Pearce got to his feet, looked down at his cum-spattered legs, and then smirked. "Nice shooting, Tex."

A laugh slipped out of Mark, surprising them both, and he grinned up at Pearce before saying in an overdone Southern drawl, "Thanks, pardner."

Pearce picked up his discarded pants and, with only his shirt covering him, tipped his head toward the steps. "Come on, let's go up and shower. Afterward we can go down to the beach and watch the moon come up."

Mark pulled on his shorts before grabbing the bottle of wine and both glasses. He followed Pearce up the steps, enjoying the view as Pearce's ass clenched and released just a few inches in front of him.

Oh yes, things were going to be all right.

CHOKED UP

Keep reading for a preview of *Choked Up*,
book four in the Up to Trouble series.

CHOKED UP
CHAPTER ONE

A loud crash from behind Mark made him jump, and he just managed to hold in a startled shout. Tension made his neck crackle like bubble wrap as he snapped his head around. An elderly woman stood a dozen feet away along the grocery aisle, staring at the floor and the mess she had created when she dropped a jar of pickles.

"Oh shit and hellfire," the woman muttered and looked over at him. "My arthritis is flaring up again."

Mark was afraid if he tried to say anything he'd only scream. He pressed his lips tight together and simply nodded before turning away. He squeezed his eyes shut and clasped the plastic handle of his shopping cart as he took slow, measured breaths.

A store employee approached the elderly woman, and their conversation faded to a distant drone as he breathed. In and out, in and out, in and out, easing his breathing and heart rate back to normal. As he worked on his breathing, Mark thought the words that had become a kind of mantra for him: *You're safe, you're well, and they cannot harm you.*

When he had managed to calm himself, Mark looked over his

shoulder again. A young man wearing a store-branded shirt was holding a mop handle and pushing a bucket on wheels down the aisle toward him. The elderly woman had moved on, leaving behind scattered pickles, broken glass, and the sharp odor of brine and garlic.

A greasy film of sweat had broken out over the length of Mark's body. Memories stormed the walls he had spent months constructing. Most were held back, but a few slipped through his defenses and put him right back on the island of Barbados in that dangerous situation that had almost cost him his freedom and, most likely, his life.

As always, the first memory to slip through his defenses was when he had walked around the corner of the bar. Without a second thought, he'd called out to the men who stood in an ominous group around a young girl. He should have left without saying a word, just gone right to the police to report the attack. But he had reacted without thinking, as usual, and he had suffered for it. He and Pearce both had suffered.

Mark realized he was scratching at the tiny scar in the crook of his left elbow, the remnant of a drug-delivering IV needle, and forced himself to stop. He gripped the handle of the shopping cart again, drew in another deep breath, and took that most difficult first step to put himself back in motion. He needed to finish his shopping and then get himself back to the apartment and start on dinner. Pearce would be home soon, and Mark liked to have dinner waiting when he arrived. He figured it was the least he could do since he hadn't been able to work for the last several months.

He was still a little distracted as he pushed his cart up and down aisles for the last few items on his list. When he reached for things, he noticed a slight tremor in his hand. His nerves felt as if they jittered just beneath the surface of his skin, and his senses had all sharpened to the point of distraction. Conversations and the noise of people coughing from other aisles sounded intrusive, and the lighting seemed brighter. But Mark forged ahead, wending his cart through the other shoppers and gritting his teeth to hold back a scream made up of equal parts rage and terror.

It was just another day.

With everything he needed finally in the buggy, he approached the registers. Anxious to be home with the doors locked and shades drawn, he got into the shortest line even though he stood behind the elderly woman who had dropped the jar of pickles. She turned to peer at him through her glasses, the lenses of which were smudged with fingerprints. Mark considered that maybe if she cleaned her glasses she might not have dropped the jar of pickles and triggered his panic attack, but then regretted the thought.

"Are you the chef in the family?" the woman asked.

Mark tried a smile, and thought he made it work, a little, even as the muscles in his belly trembled. "Yep. I decide what it'll be, buy it, and cook it."

"Do they make you clean up after, too?"

"No," Mark replied. "That he does himself."

The woman tipped her head to the side. "He?"

Mark hadn't realized he'd said it, and now his belly seemed to shrink to half its size. But, in for a penny, in for a pound.

It was a new era, after all. He and Pearce could get married if they decided to go that route, so he wiped his sweaty palms on his jeans and said, "My partner, Aaron. I cook the meals, and he cleans up afterward."

"Oh. Well, that's nice of him." She started to place her items on the conveyor belt, and Mark ran the mantra through his mind again as he looked around at the impulse buys on display near the registers. His gaze fell on a display in the main aisle behind him, which stopped him cold. Large bags of candy piled high underneath cartoon cutouts of Halloween monsters. The skin across his scalp tingled as a sudden realization stole the breath from his lungs. Halloween? Already? He pulled out his phone and checked the date. Monday, October 18. October was more than half over.

Mark turned away from the candy display and stared at the back of the elderly woman's green coat in front of him. His mind tipped and spun as he tried to think back over the months and find one bright spot, one good memory. They had returned from Barbados at the end of May. Mark had seen a doctor and then started therapy to deal with the mental fallout of his ordeal.

The weeks had bled together, becoming one long bad dream. The last several months he had talked about his abduction in Barbados so much it started to feel like a story he had heard second-hand, which happened to someone else. But the dreams always felt real, and the symptoms had never really cleared up. Post-traumatic stress disorder—PTSD in doctor speak—was the gift that just kept giving.

And now, the summer was gone, and he seemed to have just awakened and realized Halloween was coming up fast. It would be his first Halloween here in Washington, DC. Back home, he and Calvin would most likely dress in costume and hit the bars. He wasn't sure what Halloween here in DC would be like. Hell, he didn't even know if Pearce liked Halloween. And how long had it been since Mark had spoken to Calvin?

With a sudden flash of clarity, Mark realized he needed to make a change. He wasn't working; he wasn't going out unless it was for groceries or therapy. In all manner of thinking, he wasn't truly living. All he did was stay inside the apartment and rearrange his belongings. How the hell had he let things be this bad for this long?

"Aaron sounds like a keeper."

Mark blinked at the elderly woman in front of him, surprised she had spoken to him again after he'd told her he was gay.

"Pardon?"

"Your partner, Aaron," the woman said. "He sounds like a keeper."

Mark smiled, and this time it felt more true and honest on his lips. "Yeah, he is."

She returned his smile and turned away to collect her change from the cashier. As she sorted the paper money and coins into her wallet, she said, "Make sure he knows that then. Years ago, I let one slip away that I still kick myself over to this day. Hold onto him, make sure he knows he's special to you."

The sting of tears surprised Mark, but he nodded and said, "I will."

She gave a single firm nod before walking off, Mark staring after her in stunned silence.

It wasn't until later, when he parked in the lot behind their apartment that Mark realized something. Despite his panic attack in the store, this had been the first time since they returned from Barbados that he hadn't nervously watched the rearview mirror on his way home. He sat in the car and thought about his trip to the market. His reaction to the broken jar of pickles had not been as severe as what it would have been just a few weeks ago. Was all of his work in therapy sessions and on his own finally paying off?

No, it wasn't that simple. He had spent weeks, months, working through the trauma he had experienced. Right then, just that day, he felt as if he stood on the threshold of a fresh start. He might not be ready to rush out and get a job and conquer the world, but he was able to see the image of himself out in the world, willfully interacting with people.

He wasn't over it—he couldn't imagine ever being "over" what had happened to him—but today he was able to entertain the possibility that at some point in the near future, he wouldn't be acting like a shut in.

A car pulled into the parking space beside his, startling Mark out of his contemplation. His pulse quickened, and he grabbed hold of the steering wheel as he pressed his feet against the floorboard. His muscles tightened as he turned to stare at the driver. His mind ticked through self-defense moves he'd learned in a class they'd taken over the summer, and avenues for escape flickered through his mind. The new arrival was a stocky man with curly hair worn a little long, someone Mark had seen around the building since he had moved in, and he relaxed a little. Mark gave the man a brief nod and quick smile before looking down at his phone as if reading a message, though he simply sat and stared at the time on the lock screen. He waited until the man had let himself in the building before he put his head back and released the breath he'd been holding.

So, he had made some progress today, but he still had a ways to go. Mark took a few deep breaths before getting out of the car. He grabbed the bags from the backseat, tried to resist looking around the parking lot, but finally broke down and paused to sweep his gaze over the few cars in the lot. He could discern no visible threat, so he walked at a brisk pace to the door. His keys were already in hand, and he had the door open and stepped through within seconds.

The hallway closed around him, smaller, familiar, easier to deal with, and Mark licked his dry lips as he headed for the steps. His anxiety lessened as he climbed the steps to the third floor, and by the time he'd let himself into the apartment, the sweat on his palms and down the length of his back was already starting to dry. He checked the time and fought back a twitch of anxiety. He had put off the trip to the grocery store too long, nervous about leaving the apartment, and because of that he was behind on dinner preparations. Making dinner was the least he could do for Pearce, who protected him. Well, hell, it was more than that. Pearce had saved his fucking life more than once, and all Mark had done was move in and disrupt Pearce's life.

"Stop it," Mark scolded himself. "Focus on the positive. Put aside the negative."

He unpacked the grocery items and set to work, keeping an eye on the clock so he could shower before Pearce got home. He didn't want the stale stink of fear sweat on him.

Follow the link to find *Choked Up* at a number of book retailers:
https://books2read.com/chokedup

ABOUT THE AUTHOR

Hank Edwards (he/him) has been writing gay fiction for more than twenty years. He has published over forty novels and novellas and dozens of short stories. His writing crosses many sub-genres, including contemporary romance, rom-com, paranormal, suspense, mystery, wacky comedy, and erotica. He has written a number of series such as the funny and spooky Critter Catchers, Old West historical horror of Venom Valley, suspenseful FBI and civilian Up to Trouble, and the erotic and funny Fluffers, Inc. Under the pen name R. G. Thomas, he has written a young adult urban fantasy gay romance series called The Town of Superstition. He was born and still lives in a northwest suburb of the Motor City, Detroit, Michigan.

For more information:
www.hankedwardsbooks.com
hankedwardsbooks@gmail.com
www.facebook.com/groups/hankshangout

ALSO BY HANK EDWARDS

<u>Critter Catchers Series</u>

Terror by Moonlight

Chasing the Chupacabra

Swamped by Fear

The Devil of Pinesville

Screams of the Season

Horror at Hideaway Cove

Dread of Night

Critter Catchers Box Set 1

Critter Catchers Box Set 2

<u>Critter Catchers Universe Stories</u>

The Mystery of the Morelock Motel

<u>Critter Catchers: Level Up Series</u>

Grave Danger

Wet Screams

<u>Williamsville Inn Gay Romance:</u>

Snowflakes and Song Lyrics

The Cupid Crawl

Fake Date Flip-Flop

Star-Spangled Showdown

<u>**Lacetown Murder Mysteries**</u>

(co-written with Deanna Wadsworth)

Murder Most Lovely

Murder Most Deserving

<u>**Venom Valley Series**</u>

Cowboys & Vampires

Stakes & Spurs

Blood & Stone

<u>**Up to Trouble Series**</u>

Holed Up

Shacked Up

Roughed Up

Choked Up

<u>**Fluffers, Inc. Series**</u>

Fluffers, Inc.

A Carnal Cruise

Vancouver Nights

<u>**Standalone Gay Romance**</u>

Buried Secrets

Destiny's Bastard

Hired Muscle

Plus Ones

Repossession is 9/10ths of the Law

Wicked Reflection

<u>**Holiday Gay Romance:**</u>

A Gift for Greg (A Story Orgy Single)

Mistletoe at Midnight (A Story Orgy Single)

The Christmas Accomplice

<u>**Story Orgy Singles Gay Romance**</u>:

A Gift for Greg

By the Book

Cross Country Foreplay

Mistletoe at Midnight

The Cheapskate: Bad Boyfriends

With This Ring

The Story Orgy Singles Boxed Set

<u>**The Town of Superstition (YA urban fantasy series)**</u>
<u>**Published under pen name R. G. Thomas**</u>

The Midnight Gardener

The Well of Tears

The Battle of Iron Gulch

A Tangle of Secrets

<u>**Gay Erotic Short Story Collections**</u>:

A Very Dirty Dozen

Another Very Dirty Dozen

A Third Very Dirty Dozen

A Fourth Very Dirty Dozen

<u>**Salacious Singles Gay Erotic Short Stories**</u>:

Bear Market

Convoy

Double Down

Exchange Rate

Finding North

Hotel Dick

Kindred Spirits

Sacked

Stroking Midnight

Vanity Loves Company

Wet Lands